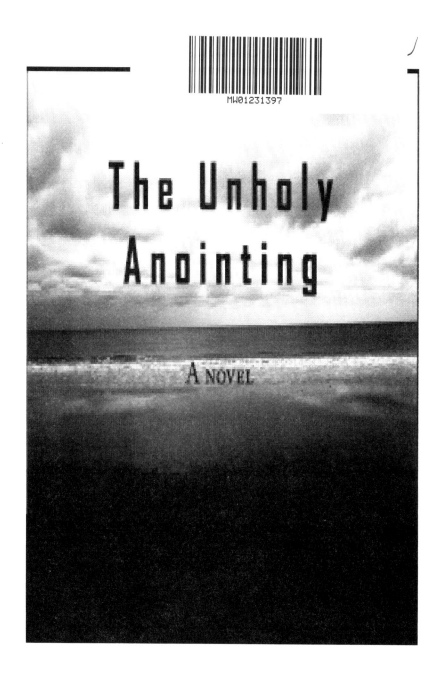

The Unholy Anointing

A NOVEL

H. A. Lewis

AuthorHouse™
1663 Liberty Drive, Suite 200
Bloomington, IN 47403
www.authorhouse.com
Phone: 1-800-839-8640

AuthorHouse™ UK Ltd.
500 Avebury Boulevard
Central Milton Keynes, MK9 2BE
www.authorhouse.co.uk
Phone: 08001974150

First published by AuthorHouse 7/24/2006

ISBN: 1-4259-4537-6 (sc)

Printed in the United States of America
Bloomington, Indiana

This book is printed on acid-free paper.

This book has been revised in 2007 and offered through
H.A.Lewis Ministries

Revised Printing
Faith Printing, Franklin Illinois

Acts 26:16

*But rise, and stand upon thy feet, for I have
appeared unto thee for this purpose, to make
thee
a minister and a witness both of these things
which thou has seen, and of those things
in the which I will appear unto thee.*

Acknowledgements

My deepest thanks to my Lord Jesus Christ for his mercies and saving grace; for without, this story would have ended a lot different.

To my beloved wife, who faithfully stands by my side through this Christian walk of faith. There seems to be more tears than smiles; but she remains faithful to God and me. I am most thankful for that. She is my best friend.

To my children, Christopher and Tricia whom I have deep high regards for who have sacrificed their childhood for the sake of our maturity and walk through the ministry. My sincere love to their families, that whatever they do, they will be blessed.

A special love and sincere thanks to all my personal friends and loved ones who have sincerely prayed and supported my family and opened up their ministries and homes to us.

Thank you for my special friends who have helped me with this book

Thank you to my kind and dear friends in the media and television business who opened the door to allow me to share my "Testimony of Victory;" in front of thousands of people in order to set those in captivity free. I am forever grateful. Thank you for believing in me.

To Laird Landis: Thank you for the revision of this book a second time

Contents

1	BIRTH OF THE PROMISED ONE	1
2	A MIRACLE	5
3	THE MEETING	11
4	WARNING	17
5	DEATH COMES	23
6	CROSS ROADS	27
7	BEATRICE AND JAMES	33
8	GOOD- BYE MOM	37
9	LEAVING THE ARMS OF LOVE	43
10	BIG TRANSITION	47
11	ATTEMPTED EXORCISM	53
12	SEASON OF PEACE	57
13	MEET DEBRA!	61
14	SCHOOL BEGINS	67
15	THE LESSON	73
16	COUNSELOR	77
17	THE ENCOUNTER	85
18	DADDY DON'T SEND ME AWAY	93
19	STRATEGY	99
20	PROJECTS -- A WHOLE NEW WORLD	105
21	LOSS OF A FRIEND	113
22	PROVEN WORTHY	119
23	A LITTLE BIT OF SUNSHINE	127
24	WORDS OF LOVE	131
25	ANOTHER INVITATION	139
26	NEED FOR DISCIPLINE	149
27	A WAY OUT- SHIPS AHOY!	151
28	NEW CHURCH EXPERIENCE	161
29	HOMEWARD BOUND	167

30	THE ANSWER COMES	175
31	POWER-THE UNHOLY ANOINTING	181
32	IT IS FINISHED!	191
33	THERE IS FREEDOM! -FREEDOM REIGNS IN ME!	199

Prologue

The woman was beyond exhaustion. This was undoubtedly the worst day of her young life. She just learned of Andy's death! Not only was she haunted by the untimely and strangely violent death of her infant son's father! But the dire warning Beatrice professed struck deep in her heart!

Her mind was racing with confusion! She just needed to sleep a little while. She just needed to relax. Maybe she'd be able to enjoy the World Series with her husband later that night.

Her eyes were finally closing and she began to sink into a deep sleep.

Suddenly! A massive pain erupted in her chest! Tears filled her eyes. A terrifying thought overcame her mind!

"OH GOD!" Beatrice was right! Her life was a horrible lie! Now it was too late for her!"

The fragile young woman's mind, soul and even her blood screamed as her heart exploded!

"God! If You are real, please help my son!"

THE BIRTH OF THE PROMISED ONE

Her name was Mary. The pains were increasing in frequency and intensity. She was in the latter stages of pregnancy. The joy of knowing she'd, shortly, be giving birth to a special son made them bearable. Who would've ever believed she'd be the chosen vessel of honor? *She will bring forth a male child who will become a God*! The moon was full and blood red on this warm late spring evening. The elders gathered in a circle around the young girl who'd just given birth. The master will be pleased. His son arrived into the world, safely. In a few years, when he comes of age, the miraculous incarnation will take place. The master, at last, will manifest in the flesh! His desire will be accomplished! He will no longer have to work through weak vessels of clay. He can directly do his will through his son, without the hindrance of any human will! The elders laid their hands on the infant. They imparted blessings and power to the chosen one.

This night is the fulfillment of the promised prophesies of the one who is to come. *It is the responsibility of the promised one to join all divided factions of all nations together in unity to be one mighty force in order to establish his father's kingdom here on earth.* For now, the boy must be protected. He must be hidden! The enemy and his followers

1

must be prevented from finding him. They will stop the promise of the chosen one from being fulfilled if they have an opportunity! They will destroy him if given the slightest chance. Even before he can come into the fullness of his power!

Three months came and went since the birth of the chosen one. On that glorious night tears were produced from an emotional cocktail of joy and pain. Pain, from the labor of childbirth, which resulted in great joy, knowing the *chosen one* had arrived!

Tears once again ran down Mary's face; but not from injury or pain. The tears ran freely now for great sorrow. The child, the promised one, lay dying in the hands of medical experts. The best the world has to offer, yet there is nothing they can do to help him! The elderly doctor looked with great concern at the young couple standing before him. He spoke gently, but firmly. "Mary." he confessed. "There's nothing we can do. He's beyond our medical help. Go home. When his time comes, we'll call. It should be within the hour."

"How can this be happening?" Mary cried! Her mind was drowning in confusion. Are not all powers, rulers and principalities under submission to the great lord? Does not sickness obey his command and leave at his word? Isn't her son the chosen one? Is it not he who is chosen to become the incarnation of the great god? Isn't god's kingdom to be established through this child? He is destined to bring unity to all the factions of the believers! If this is so, then why has this curse come upon my child? Isn't he the only begotten son? Is it because the master is somehow angry with the followers and finds them unworthy of the gift? Is he going to take the child back and wait for a more worthy group? She had to know the answer! She was devastated and confused. She spoke to her husband and kindly asked him to go home and wait. "When it's over Martin, I'll come home."

2

The man obediently left. He had no idea what was truly happening. He wasn't a believer and was in the dark about the child. He thought the boy was his! He had no idea who the child's real father was. Mary went out in the pouring rain. Luckily, there was a large window where she could look in at the nursery and her poor infant son. Mary stood in the dark, rain drenching her long black hair. She was praying softly as she stared into the window of the nursery. Praying alone for the lone infant left abandoned on the steel gurney. Will he live or die?

Mary cried out, again in absolute agony! "Why must this child die?" It wasn't right! How could the master's will be fulfilled if his only begotten son is dead? Time is of the essence. He can't afford to postpone an event of this nature until sometime in the far future. The enemy and His followers could find out and do great harm to the master's plan. Although the enemy will never truly defeat the great lord, He might, at least, be able to postpone the master's wonderful ultimate plan for one world government and universal peace. "Mary! Mary!" The voice of the great one cried out with fullness of compassion and sympathy. "Why do you stand here crying in the rain?"

"Oh master." proclaimed Mary, dropping to her knees in holy awe and reverence, "Our son lies alone, dying. The great hope of this world. The chosen one will soon be gone and the world will once again be consumed with despair. Master, lord, my beloved, Why? Oh, why must this child die? You know all things and all things are subject to you. Why must your only son, our only hope, be taken from a world that needs him so much? You are the god of this world and the mighty prince of the power of the air. All creation trembles at your voice. Will you not spare your own son?"

Her master replied, "Mary, haven't I given so much to this world already? Now you want me to give these unworthy ones my only son? They don't truly love him! They ask of me to give to them, but they never freely give to me. Now, you want me to give my son, freely, so they can grow rich and

3

prosperous and rule the world? I am not as foolish as the enemy. I will not give my son freely! My people must be willing to pay the price. There is no free ride with me. What would they be willing to give me to keep my son here?"

Mary answered without hesitating. "Lord I will willingly give my life to you for his; with no regrets! Take me now and let our son live so you may be glorified! I want your will accomplished through his life. His destiny must be fulfilled!"

The master smiled at Mary and proclaimed. "So be it! Go your way, woman. Our son shall live as you asked. Know this. There shall come a day when I shall claim your offering. Remember, also, there is no increase of power without the shedding of blood! Either your blood or the blood of this child! ***Blood must be shed!"***

2
A MIRACLE

Mary went home at the master's command. She was barely home for an hour when the phone rang. It was the doctor. "Hello Mary. This is Dr. Costa, from Mercy Hospital. Something extremely strange and wonderful has happened!" confessed a perplexed Dr. Costa. "You and your husband can collect the boy and bring him home!" After a pause he asked, "Mary, are you a woman of faith? Do you believe in a higher power? There can be no other explanation for your son's healing. It's a genuine miracle! If I were you, I'd already be on my way to church to give thanks."

Mary answered the doctor. "I've already done so. I made sure the one responsible for this miracle receives the praise." The child was finally home, but something was wrong. He seemed to have great difficulty moving his legs. And he didn't cry. The medical experts told his parents he was more than fortunate to be alive. He suffered an extremely lethal case of spinal meningitis. It should have taken his life! He will not speak. He will not walk normally. Unfortunately, this form of meningitis left him crippled for life.
Mary once again cried out to the great lord. "Why have you allowed this to happen to our son? He is the promised one, the

5

establisher, meant for greatness! How will he ever rule if he can't speak or walk? Who will follow a cripple? The followers of the master are people who follow after strength and power. Their minds are strong as well as their spirits. They believe only the strong have the right to survive. The weak and the infirm must be destroyed. It is the law! Now, the so-called chosen one is infirm. How could this happen? What is the purpose? Is the enemy strong enough to do this? Did He find the promised one and in His jealousy of the master, lash out at our son? Where are the guardians assigned to protect the child? Where is his great familiar? Were they not ordered by you, my master in order to protect the child at all cost? Their failure must mean their very existence is forfeit!"

Again, the master spoke. "Mary, why do you doubt my wisdom? Did you not give this child to me? Is he not mine to do with as I please? **Does he not bear *my* mark on his forearm? That mark was placed on him while in his mother's womb.** Then, why do you question? You asked for his life. That was all I promised! I gave him back to you as I said I would. If I choose to return him damaged, that is my choice. Don't ever challenge my ways again! All that matters is my will be done! Anyone who gets in my way shall be cut off! That includes you, Mary! Is my meaning clear?"

"Yes, master." Mary fearfully replied. "Forgive me my doubts; only your will truly matters."

"Mary, I knew you'd see it my way. Now remember your blood offering. The day is coming when I will require it of you!" After he left, Mary began, for the first time in her young life, to seriously question what the master told her. Confusion filled her mind. Wasn't her mother a faithful follower of the master, as well as her grandmother? There were six generations who served him. Wasn't her son the beginning of the blessed seventh generation of faithful followers? Yet, didn't her mother and grandmother die mysteriously? Their deaths couldn't be explained; even by the medical examiner! Their bodies were so grotesquely bruised on the outside. They were completely black and blue. They looked as if they had been brutally beaten. Their hair had completely fallen out! The doctors' diagnosis was a stoppage of the heart. The examiner declared there was no heart! How could that be? He swore there were no cuts on the body anywhere! The doctors had no explanation for the deaths. Officially, they would only say they were abnormal. Some of the most mysterious facts surrounding the deaths of grandma at forty-two and mom at thirty-two, seemed amazing. Was this just a coincidence between these deaths? There seemed to be no break in the lineage. Each one faced the same death. What was she to believe? Was she next? Mary was almost twenty-two! Was this the price of serving the master?

The family was so dedicated and faithful in their belief. All except for Mary's father. He was a self-centered drunk, caring for no one other than himself. Mary had to raise her brothers and sisters herself after her mother died. Her father would lock up the food. No one could have any. Every winter he'd have himself arrested so he wouldn't have to listen to Mary and the children complaining about being cold and hungry. If it weren't for Martin coming into her life, she and her brothers and sisters would probably have starved to death! She was only 14 when she met him. Mary felt the higher power had put them together. He loved their son and truly believed the boy was his child. Martin would do anything for her and the children. He was not a follower of the master. In fact, he was very confused and believed the opposite. He was a naïve and simple man who saw the enemy as a good and caring God. He believed the master was created by God and rebelled against Him. This caused a war in the heavenlies. The master was thrown out, along with one third of his brothers; all at the hands of Michael. Martin had to be kept in the dark about Mary's true belief. He'd never understand.

The heavy burden she was carrying caused her to drink more and more. The stress was too much for her to handle alone. She was consuming two six packs of beer and a bottle of wine; just to make it through a single day! Her life was full of fear and misery. Where was the joy and peace the master had promised?

Many things he promised never came to pass. Mary couldn't remember ever really being happy. No one, outside of Martin, had truly loved or cared about her.

Oh, there was Andy, Mary's boyfriend. He was the father of her daughter Tina; whom Martin thought was his daughter. Mary knew Andy didn't really love her. He was just interested in sex. Andy was also a follower. Mary could discuss the faith with him, though. This was very important to her. It was getting harder and harder to take everything by faith. Mary's world was coming down around her. Everything Mary was taught about the master now seemed to be a big, beautiful, created lie. It was a story created to cover the truth. Wasn't it written in the enemy's book that the master could appear as an angel of light and his followers as servants of light? Was not the master called a deceiver and the father of lies and a murderer and thief? Was this true? Could Mary and her entire family be deceived? If this were so, then she was in extreme danger for her very life and soul. The life of her son was in serious danger, also. She couldn't turn to the God of the Christians, for she'd forsaken Him ever since she could remember. If she did turn to Him, her family would turn their back on her.

For Mary, there was no other choice but the master's way. This lifestyle, *la vecchia religione*, was handed down to her through five generations. She was warned never to leave it! Maybe this feeling was just depression. She was the mother of three young children. She was taking care of her four younger siblings. Now, less than a year after nearly losing her first son she was carrying another! She was only 22! But felt very old. Surely, the master was all he claimed to be. She was just going through an emotional time brought on by all this stress. This will pass and Mary will recover. She only hoped the master wouldn't sense her doubts and fears. He will not tolerate any disbelief in any way. The master can be cruel. Mary had seen the punishment first hand, exacted on those who displeased him. She didn't want to join that number. As another rush of doubt flooded her mind and emotions with painful memories, she remembered her encounter with Dr. Costa a year before.

Once again, Mary found herself staring into the face of Dr. Costa. "Mary." said Dr. Costa. "I'm so sorry to have to tell you this. The child died right after birth. There wasn't a thing we could do to save him. His heart wasn't developed. His lungs weren't even formed."

Mary wept. The birth of Michael was so very important to her. She would have finally been able to present Martin with a son who was truly his! It would have been a way of paying him back for all he had done for her. But Martin never had the chance to hold his own son. Life could be so cruel and unfair. The master claimed he was all-powerful. He claimed he loved her and his followers. Where was he when Mary needed him? Why did he always allow terrible things to happen? Why did he refuse to answer the questions, which pierced through Mary's heart?

3
THE MEETING

Mary watched her small son as he dragged himself across the floor. The child couldn't crawl, but it didn't prevent him from getting around. He didn't cry or make any sound. It was as if he had no vocal cords. In spite of these weaknesses, the child seemed to enjoy life. He would sit for hours watching his sister's run and laugh. He seemed to share in their fun, even though he couldn't partake in it. Mary wondered what the child would say if he could speak. He was only two years old. His eyes were uniquely intense. There seemed to be so much life behind them! Mary held the child, closely. She told him of her master's great purpose and interest in the boy and of her great god.

The master came back only once after Mary willfully committed to sacrifice herself so that he would spare the child's life. He didn't speak to Mary. He only stared at the child. The only audible words seemed to be cruel and heartless. He softly whispered with a rasping voice, "No one will suspect a helpless cripple to be of any use to anyone. Never mind being the fulfillment of the promise!" It seemed to Mary, the master caused the boy to be sick for his own purpose. This way he could control him and govern him. The masters' own son meant nothing to him. All that truly mattered was the completion of his glorious plan. The master would rule this

11

world and all therein; no matter what. Even the enemy, the so-called God of creation, couldn't stop him.

Without even a glance at Mary, the master bellowed a horrible laugh. She'd never heard anything like it. Her heart filled with fear for her son and her own life! The master vanished! Mary began to shake and cry. She felt so helpless and confused. Her life was falling apart. She drank more and more, just to make it through the day. Her nights were filled with horror. Her dreams were nightmares. The master appeared in her dreams, at times. She saw him as a terrible creature; a monster that sought only to steal, kill and destroy. These dreams revealed him as a powerful, rebellious creature divested of all privileges. He was cast out of the enemy's kingdom. Mary's world and all she believed was now being ripped apart at the seams! She was even showing signs of doubt! Mary needed to talk to Andy! So much was going on. But he hadn't attended the last two meetings. Rumors were starting to spread. He'd been seen in the company of two traitors who were now followers of the enemy!

Mary finally had a chance to speak with Andy. He shared that what he was doing was wrong. He won't participate any longer. He quit hiding. He's taking responsibility for his own life! He told her his eyes were being opened to Truth. Mary warned him to be careful about what he was saying and whom he was saying it to. If the master ever found out, he'd think this an act of rebellion. Andy would pay a dear price for his freedom. Then Andy shared the strangest thing she'd ever heard. He said, "I'm no longer afraid of him. The only thing he can do is destroy my body. Now, he can never destroy my soul or my new spirit! For One greater owned them." He embraced Mary one last time in his tender arms. He said, "Mary, meet me tomorrow night. There's something I must show you! For your sake and for the child's, you must meet me! Both your lives are in terrible danger, as is your eternal destiny!"

~ A Family Tradition ~

After speaking with Mary, Andy went home to his small apartment. He thought about his life; especially what happened to him in the last few weeks! Andy was raised in the way of *Strega, a Blood Witch*. It was his family's tradition; 'la vecchia religione!' It was the only way he knew. The power passed on from his mother to his sister at midnight on her 21st birthday. This was the custom. He was methodically shown the old ways. He was taught all about the old gods and goddesses. He was dedicated to the master as a child. He was one of the master's **hunters**! Hunters were dedicated to seek out and destroy those who left the way. These missions troubled him. It was while he struggled with these thoughts that he encountered the two traitors. This resulted in the dramatic changes in his life over the last few weeks! Very little was truly known about Andy. The followers really didn't know him. There were many rumors about him, but no one doubted his loyalty. It was at one of the meetings where Andy and Mary met and fell in love. He did love Mary. But when the master claimed her, he broke off the relationship. He didn't want to offend him. A surprise came at one of the meetings. The master placed them together as a couple, with his blessing! After this, he was even more dedicated to the master! Many of the followers believed Andy owned a large panther as a familiar. They didn't know the large beast, seen in his apartment, was not his familiar. It was Andy! This was his hunter form!

~ A Plan for world control ~

Andy was what the unlearned called a shape shifter or were-beast. The followers called it a hunter. Only the most loyal of believers, who were truly, fanatically dedicated to the master, could ever reach this level. It is believed once you reach this spiritual level, you can never turn back! This is almost always true. Rarely does a hunter ever leave the family!

Two weeks earlier Andy was on a mission. He was tracking the traitorous couple that'd left the coven and joined the enemy's side. They not only left the master but also were betraying his plan for world control! This could not be allowed to happen! Andy set out on the mission; business as usual. He wasn't prepared for what happened next! Andy sat in the enemy's churches before and never had a problem. Most of the enemies' followers couldn't back up their words with their deeds. Few were even familiar the Book they held so dear. It seemed a mere religious act they did. The enemy's Book contained great power if believed in and spoken. The Book they held was like no other. In fact, Andy knew it better than most! This ability helped him to destroy six churches from within, using only gossip and rumors! Andy finally spotted the conspiring couple as they were getting out of their car. They were about to enter a small church where they intended to share their story. It was perfect. The parking lot was filled with vehicles, but everybody was inside waiting for the couple. They were alone, vulnerable and still a distance away from the safety of the church. As Andy started to approach them, he began to feel a change within him. *He was transforming into the spirit that lies within him, **the Black Panther**!*

As they approached the church, the couple felt compelled to turnaround. They were astonished by what they saw! But, instead of running, the man simply stepped in between the beast and his wife. Supernatural courage filled his heart! Strangely, the beast sensed no fear in either of them. He confronted a great power he had never known. Before the panther could react and attack, the man stepped forward and firmly, but gently spoke. He proclaimed in the name of the Lord, Most High! He faced Andy pronouncing, "You are be bound where you stand! I command you to return to your natural form; in Jesus name!" The panther was instantly seized in a grip so strong he couldn't move forward or backward. The spiritual eyes of the animal were opened and he beheld two very large angels; fiery messengers of the enemy. These warriors were standing on each side of the man and woman with their huge swords drawn! The panther knew this battle was over. The man spoke again in that same firm, but gentle voice. Andy felt himself compelled to obey his command! The panther changed back into Andy's real self. Andy noticed something very strange. He couldn't explain it. But he couldn't sense any anger, fear or bitterness in the couple, only compassion. The man spoke kindly to Andy. He said they were waiting for him. Their Lord told them earlier, Andy would be coming that night to kill them. He wanted to stop them from sharing their testimony. They asked their God for mercy to be shown to Andy. For wasn't he deceived even as they had been? The couple pleaded and prayed that Andy would be given one more chance to know the Lord Jesus as his Savior.

Andy was irresistibly drawn by the words of this gentle man and could do nothing but follow him into the small church. He sat glued to the seat as the couple shared their story of life among the master's followers. They praised God and said God loved them; even when they were His enemies! He learned, through Christ's shed blood he was set free! He learned by the grace of God's Spirit and the authority in the name of His Son Jesus, he could walk in victory! Without embarrassing Andy or pointing him out to the people, the man spoke to him and offered him the same gift of freedom he and his wife had received. He offered Andy forgiveness of sins, reconciliation with God, and eternal salvation, which is available through Jesus Christ, alone! Andy felt himself responding, willingly, to the invitation.

No one, outside of the couple and the angels, knew the intensity of the miracle occurring that night when Andy walked to the altar. He, who changed into a beast at will, had been transformed by a greater power, into a Son of God. He was adopted into the beloved. He was renewed into the image of God's only Son. A multitude of angels in heaven rejoiced in the presence of God! Andy didn't go home for the next two weeks. He stayed with the couple and learned as much as he could about his new Master. The Christian life he now knew and felt; was so overwhelming for him! He just had to share his new relationship and experience!

15

He had to tell Mary! He needed to share the truth about what he just found out. He realized her son was not a god nor the Son of God, but the victim of the father of lies. Her very life and soul, as well as the child's, were in lethal danger unless she escaped to the One she called the enemy. Andy knew only the Christ could help her now. Andy confided in the couple. He told them what he was going to do. They did not try to stop him. They prayed for him and asked God to keep his soul safe. Andy tried to meet with Mary but the next meeting would never take place.

When Mary arrived at Andy's home the police were already there. A large crowd gathered outside the apartment house. Mary approached one of the people and asked what was going on. Apparently a young man was found beaten to death in his apartment. The police were baffled since the doors were all locked tight. They said he had a shotgun lying across his lap he never used. He looked as if someone had beaten him to death with a baseball bat. Where he sat! Mary knew, without even looking at him. It was Andy! Her eyes filled with tears as she turned to make her way home. Mary's life became even more miserable; realizing she lost her best friend. Her husband could never understand her as Andy had.

The master had not returned. Her son was still in bad shape, without any improvement, physically. What was she going to do? This situation couldn't become any worse, she thought. She was starting up to her second floor apartment in a daze. Out of the fog of her mind she thought she heard a voice speaking to her. Mary looked up and saw her neighbor coming toward her. She had hardly spoken a word to her before because Beatrice was a follower of the enemy. But Mary's faith was failing. She desperately needed someone; anyone to talk to and Beatrice called her name...

Could Beatrice be the answer to her cry?

4
WARNING

"**H**ello Mary!" said Beatrice. "How are you feeling, dear? I'm so sorry to hear what happened to your friend Andy. He was so young. He had so much going for him. I was so pleasantly surprised, though, to have seen him at church! His testimony of deliverance was so wonderful and powerful. Some of the subjects he shared were so deep; it was hard to believe these things really happen! I was blown away when he shared about being a shape shifter, or as he referred to it, a hunter! Mary, you know, most of the people in our little church can't believe a man can do something like that! But Satan is powerful and without Christ no man can stand against him. I believe Andy knows his Lord, now and I'm at peace with his future." What Beatrice said next caused Mary to tremble uncontrollably. Beatrice simply stated, "Oh thank God for the precious Blood of the Lamb and the wonderful Name of Jesus. His mercy endures forever!" Mary began to shake uncontrollably and fear suddenly came upon her! Beatrice asked, "What's wrong, Mary?"

Mary growled in an ominous voice, but not her own! "Do not use that name or mention the Blood in my presence, ever! Go away, you foolish woman and leave me alone! There is nothing your Christ can do for me!"

17

Fear even came over Beatrice, momentarily, until the Word of God she trusted was brought to mind. She was reminded; *'greater is He that is in you, than He that is in the world.'* Beatrice replied with a calm, but firm voice, proclaiming, "The Lord has promised and He has given every believer power over anything which would exalt itself against God! Be thou gone! Thou lying spirit! Thou shall not hinder my Lord's work He hath prepared for me to do. Mary shall hear the Truth today!"

Mary was shaking terribly, unable to respond. Yet this terrifying voice, which sounded like the master, was speaking through her. Threatening Beatrice! Mary could sense that whoever this spirit was, he was afraid of this little woman. Once again Beatrice firmly commanded the spirit to leave 'by the Blood of the Lamb and in the Name of Jesus, the Christ.' Instantly! Mary stopped shaking and felt the presence leave her body. She collapsed against the wall to support herself. She felt so tired and drained. All her energy seemed to drain from her body. Mary just wanted to get away. Mary was exhausted. She wanted to go home. She tried to push Beatrice aside but the little woman wouldn't let her. "Mary!" she exclaimed, "You must listen to me! Your life, and the child's life, depends on the decision you make today! It is no coincidence we meet today. It's no coincidence Andy was just in our church. The Lord sent me to speak to you. The devil is deceiving you and has ensnared your very soul! If you don't denounce him and come to the Lord, quickly, then I fear a great doom awaits you in eternity! What happened to Andy could happen to you, and worse? Do you understand me?"

Mary shouted, "No! You're a liar! The master, my god, loves our son and me. It is your God who is cruel and binds you. He's narrow-minded and places unbearable burdens on you. Ever since the Garden of Eden! He's been afraid of man becoming just like Him since the Tower. The master told us the same truth he told Eve. We are all gods and someday we'll rule with the master. The master gives us freedom and helps us to evolve into our godship; while your God puts a bunch of religious do's and don'ts on you. He tries to keep you in bondage. He wants to prevent you from becoming the god you are. Because the master loves us so much; he had to tell us this great revelation! This is what caused your so-called God of Love to be filled with jealous anger and separate from the master. Unlike the fable you believe, our master was not thrown out of your mystical heaven by your factorial Michael, but instead, of his own free will, he chose to come and dwell among man, to help us evolve into the gods we truly are now! Beatrice, what do you have to say to that?"

Beatrice replied, "Oh Mary! How wrong you are, dear child. In the beginning, God formed man out of the dust of the earth. Man was made in the image of God and became a living soul when God breathcd the Breath of Life into him. From the side of man, woman was taken and made to be the man's helpmate. They were both lovingly placed in the garden. God, being the God of love, gave man free will; just as He did with the angels. God doesn't want robots that are forced to obey Him. He wants free souls who freely choose to love and serve Him from love and their grateful hearts. God created your master and much was given to him. He was an anointed Cherub, greater than all other creation and the sum of beauty and wisdom was in him. But he became full of pride and wanted all to bow to him including God, the one who created him!"

~~ He is known as Satan ~~

"He was known as Lucifer, the Light Bearer. He deceived o. third of the angels; leading them in rebellion against God. Michael, the great prince over Israel, fought against him and his army and cast him out of heaven. He now abides in the atmosphere. He is known as Satan, the Accuser of the brethren, the Deceiver, the god of this world, and the prince of the power of the air. Now child, please listen! He's not satisfied with the trouble he caused in heaven. His wrath and vengeance are insatiable! He's come to earth to tempt God's greatest creation, created in His own image; to destroy the relationship between the Creator and His creation in retaliation to God. When he entered into the Shining One, he deceived Eve; who in turn

19

caused her husband to fall. God gave ownership, authority and responsibility over all the earth to Adam. Because dominion over the world was given to Adam; sin entered the world through Adam when he sinned. When they sinned, Adam and Eve's spirits died and they lost relationship with God and the lordship of this planet. Because they disobeyed God and obeyed Satan, Adam's ownership of the earth was transferred to Satan; making Satan its new ruler! You know that to whom you present yourselves slaves to obey, you are that one's slaves whom you obey. Whether of sin leading to death, or of obedience leading to righteousness!"

"The only way man can be restored back to God, his dead spirit reborn, is through the shed blood of a righteous man. But never can one be found. So God, because of His great love for us, became a man in the flesh and dwelt a sinless life among His creation. This is what the incarnation is about, Mary. God came in the flesh as the sinless Christ, completely man and completely God. And as the Christ, He poured Himself out for us. He died for us; that we might live with Him forever! Your son is not God. He is not the savior of mankind. He is only a little boy! Satan is ensnaring him! His master will betray him. The blood of Jesus saves us, delivers us, cleanses us, heals us and restores us .The blood of your son cannot. The name of Jesus causes the demons to tremble and sets the captives free. Nothing can stand against it. Your son's name has no power. Mary please, before it's too late. Come to Jesus and accept His love into your life!"

Mary felt the dark prince re-enter her, possess her. She heard herself once again yelling in that strange, other voice. The foulest words she ever spoke to anyone were spewing from her mouth. She even heard herself threaten Beatrice with hell if she kept pleading the Blood and using the Name of Jesus! The commotion was so loud it began to draw the other neighbors out of their apartments to see what was going on. Martin arrived right in the middle of all this and took Mary by the shoulders. He pushed Beatrice away, warning her to stop all that religious garbage and leave Mary alone! Mary calmed down after Beatrice left. She confided in Martin and told him what really bothered her. She didn't understand why a lot of what Beatrice said made sense to her. A part of Mary wanted to believe it but something within her wouldn't let her. But Martin believed the Bible was true. "You know," consoled Martin, "my parents are believers. I never really followed their faith, but I never denied it either. I just don't believe in pushing anyone's personal beliefs on someone else. I guess all roads lead to Rome."

Mary looked at Martin, wishing for the first time, he would take a stand one way or the other. If he would only help make up Mary's mind. She was tired now and just wanted to go to bed. The World Series was on later that night. She wanted to watch the game. Mary felt so old. She was just twenty-two years old, but life was so hard. It was five o'clock. Maybe she needed a nap. Mary kissed Martin and asked him to wake her at 9:00 o'clock, in time for the game. Martin smiled and lovingly said, "OK kiddo, I'll see you at nine." *Neither knew this kiss was their last!*

5
DEATH COMES

Nine O'clock came and Martin entered into the bedroom to wake his lovely wife. What he saw in their bed froze his heart and changed him forever. There in the bed, in place of his lovely 22 year old wife, was her corpse; beaten beyond recognition. She was completely black and blue and all of her beautiful, long black hair had fallen out. Martin's heart felt screams of agony pierced the three floors of the apartment house. Someone called the police. They arrived and found a broken Martin on his knees, holding the hand of his young wife. He couldn't believe she was dead. Then the police noticed the condition of Mary's body. They immediately arrested Martin for the murder of his wife. Martin seemed to have answered a million questions for the police. Now he had to call someone to take care of the children while he went to the station. He was placed in a holding cell while more information was found to prove his guilt.

Meanwhile, the county coroner performed an autopsy on the body of Mary. He discovered a very strange thing. He immediately called the chief of police. He had to see him. He must see him! Right away! When the chief of police arrived, the coroner said, "Joe, this young woman could not have possibly been murdered by her husband. Something very strange and inexplicable has happened. We can't label it a

23

murder. I'm going to say she died of natural causes as a result of cardiac arrest. Her heart stopped beating."

"How do you know this?" asked the chief.

∿ Her heart was missing ∿

"Simply." replied the coroner. "When I opened her chest cavity to examine her heart, it was missing. It looked as if someone had surgically removed it from her chest. I don't know how that can happen. I just know no man killed her. There are no entry wounds on her at all!" The chief returned back to his office. He released Martin, and told him what the coroner said. Martin guessed, "Her heart exploded in her chest, probably due to the amount of drinking she's been doing lately."

The chief replied, "No. **There was no heart to be found at all! No incision was found on her body.** Not the slightest cut!" Neither man spoke. Finally the chief turned to Martin saying, "What are your plans now, Martin? You have three children of your own, plus four fairly young in-laws you've been helping."

"Well," replied Martin, "the in-laws are old enough to be on their own. My brother and his wife are taking the two girls. The lady upstairs said she'd take the boy. You know, he's the hardest to take care of because of his handicap. I don't know if he'll ever walk, and I don't believe he will ever speak. I need some time to think and to put my life together. I can't believe Mary's gone! We were just talking at 4:00pm. And by 9:00pm, she was gone, forever!"

"Chief." replied Martin, "I need to go home. If I'm free to leave, I'll be on my way."

The Chief replied, "You just need you to sign a few more forms and then you can go. I'm sorry we had to arrest you, but the situation warranted it."

24

"Its ok." replied Martin. "You were just doing your job. I would've been as suspicious as you if I were in your shoes. Where are those forms? I need to sign them so I can go back to the kids." After signing the forms, Martin headed home.

6
CROSS ROADS

The place just wasn't the same without Mary. Mary wouldn't be there any more. He'd never hear her play her music or smell her cooking his favorite foods. There'd be no laughter. It seems like the apartment became a place for the unclean. There was coldness in his home no amount of sunshine could warm up. While Martin was in jail, Beatrice took care of the apartment, making sure all of Mary's belongings were given to the Salvation Army. He didn't want any of Mary's belongings in the house when he got home. It was too painful for him to deal with any reminders, other than the memories he was carrying in his heart and his mind for her. The place was barren and cold. There wasn't enough sunshine to warm it up. Martin sat in his favorite chair. The emotions built up inside him for two day's.

He eventually released some of his pain and received some peace of mind. So many things raced around his mind. Funeral plans had to be made, and quickly. Relatives needed to be contacted. What was he going to do with his in-laws and his children? He'd been supporting them for a long time. Change for them is about to happen and they'll have to support themselves. The shock of Mary's death was finally hitting him. The responsibility was overwhelming.

27

Suddenly, a knock at the door startled him out of his deep thought. Martin opened the door. Beatrice was standing there loaded with groceries. Martin was taken by surprise at the kindness this woman had shown him and his family. Beatrice humbly spoke to him saying, "Martin, please except these groceries from James and me. We want to do what ever we can to help you. I'll bring you all a hot meal as well."

He told her his brother and wife had offered to take the two girls for as long as was necessary. "My in-laws are old enough to take care of themselves. They'll just have to leave." This left the boy to be cared for. He thanked her for the groceries and said he'd think about everything she said. He'd get back to her the next day. Martin considered his life. He considered his plans and what he wanted to do. He visited Beatrice and asked her if she and James still wanted to watch the boy for a while. He wanted one thing understood. "No matter what you think about me; just understand I love my children! If I let you take the boy, it will only be for a short time. As soon as I'm on my feet again, I'll want him back. Is that clear?"

Beatrice replied, "Yes, of course. We have children of our own, and if James were ever in your place, I hope someone would offer to help him so he wouldn't have to take the children to the state. I'll take good care of him. I'll treat him like my own."

"Thank you for your kind offer, but I need to ask you a question," replied Martin. "Please forgive me if I offend you, but why would you, a black woman, offer your help to me, a white man? Even my own people won't help?"

"Well, Martin," replied Beatrice, "it's because our God is no respecter of any man. He doesn't judge their color. When God sent His Son to die in our place, He showed the ultimate love; the greatest love. There is no black. There is no white. He died for everyone. He died for Gentiles and Jews. It made no difference to Him. He loves us all equally. All anyone has to do is accept His love. Then we become His examples."

"Now, Beatrice," replied Martin," please don't start preaching to me, again. I know you have your religion. My parents had their religion. Mary had her religion and that other society she belonged to. Religion is okay, but I'm not going to bother God with my problems. He has enough problems to deal with. I know He cares for me, but I need to handle things myself. Remember Beatrice, it's written, somewhere in the Bible, 'God helps those who help themselves.'"

"Sorry Martin, but that's not true. Nowhere in Scripture are we taught that falsehood. That is a lie from the throne of Satan himself, the father of lies! God wants us to take everything to Him in prayer. He is our Heavenly Father. He wants us to cast all our cares and burdens on Him. If we believe in His Son Jesus, as our Lord, and Savior, then we know, like any good father, He wants to help His children. Martin, please understand! Religion has done more harm to more people and led more souls to hell than all the other lies of Satan combined. Religion gives you a false sense of security based on your own good works or deeds or your relationship to another person or group."

"All roads do not lead to heaven. The only way to God, the Father is through Jesus Christ His Son, and no man can earn his way through works or deeds, so he cannot boast in himself. Please keep in mind Martin; it's only through the Holy Spirit that a man is drawn to Jesus. Its only through accepting the sacrifice and victory of Christ on the cross that a man or woman is truly born again and reconciled with God."

∼ God is not interested in religion; but in relationship ∼

"*God is not interested in religion or rituals. He's interested in relationship. This is the true source power.* My questions are simple, "Do you have a religion or a relationship with God the Father, through Jesus Christ, His Son. Does the Holy Spirit of the Living God abide within you? Can you say from your heart, Jesus is my Lord and my Savior? Do you know you are saved by His completed work? Are you led by the Holy Spirit within you?"

"Beatrice," said Martin, "thank you for your kind offer. When this child comes tomorrow, I'll let you take him for a while. Please understand; I don't have time for this religious foolishness. It's fine for you and James, if you want to believe it. I don't need a crutch to walk through life. I noticed most of the people at your church are woman and children. James seems to be one of few men who are going to your church. If this is so great, why are there so few men going? I know why Beatrice. A man doesn't need or have time for this foolishness. He is strong enough to make it on his own. You cannot trust in Him for your everyday needs. You cannot wait for pennies to come down from heaven. No one is going to make the problems of life go away for you."

"If your God was so concerned with me personally, then why did He allow Mary to die so young and leave three children without a mother? What did I do to Him? Did He have to take my wife from me? I let Mary go to mass. I even agreed to let the children be raised in the Roman Catholic Church; which was her request. I let her take the boy to those so-called secret meetings, which she didn't know I found out about. I let Mary have her religion and never interfered in any way. But what good did it do? God took her life anyway. Even though she was a religious woman! You will never convince me of God's love."

"Do I believe in God? Yes. I told you my parents are believers and raised us in the church. Do I believe God created the world? Yes. Do I believe He is personally involved with us all? No! He set things in motion. He set up the laws of creation, the universal law of matter, time and the paths of the planets. We are now left on our own until the end of time. Do I believe in the devil? Yes. He is, in theory, just a scapegoat to blame our weakness and faults on. We don't need a devil for evil to exist. Man is wicked enough on his own. In fact, we're animals with a soul, or as you religious folk believe, with an intellect, emotion, and will. Beatrice, if I'm wrong, I have my whole life ahead of me to think this religion question through. I won't bother God and therefore He won't need to bother me. That goes double for the devil."

"Martin," replied Beatrice. "I am so sorry to hear you say this. You, of all people, should know you are never guaranteed a tomorrow. Look at Mary and how young she was. Her life is over. She had no peace. Do you? God didn't take Mary to punish you. Mary's life ended because she made choices that tragically shaped and shortened her life. Martin, please hear me. I honestly believe it was due to those meetings she was attending. Didn't you find it strange that Mary and Andy were members of the same group, and they both died two weeks apart; the exact same way? The only difference was Andy left the group and embraced Jesus as Lord."

"So, Beatrice," answered Martin, "if your God is so good and so strong, why couldn't He save Andy? Didn't Andy belong to Him? Perhaps, instead of trying to recruit me to your way, you should turn to my way of thinking. Beatrice, God doesn't care one-way or the other about man. In Mary's Church, the priest teaches that God is angry with man because of his rebellion against God; and the only dealing He has with man is to punish him for his sin. They also teach that Jesus is upset because He had to be crucified for man. You see, He isn't happy with us. The only chance we have is through Mary, the mother of God, because of her compassionate heart."

"Martin." Beatrice exclaimed. "I need to interrupt. That's not true. Our Bible teaches us that *God, the Father, so loved the world that He gave his only begotten Son, so that whosoever believes in Him would be saved.* The Bible also teaches that Jesus is our Intercessor with the Father. He is always interceding for us. Mary, although blessed among woman, was still only human and she is not a co-savior or co-intercessor. She, also, was not the mother of God. God had no beginning; neither does He have an ending. She was simply the human mother of Jesus as the Son of God and Son of Man. She is the human 'vessel,' chosen by God to bear the eternal God, come to us in the flesh. At the wedding in Cana, where Jesus did His first miracle by turning the water into wine, what did Mary tell the servants?" Martin thought a moment and said, "Not what she said, but what He said!"

"Martin, I know you are hurt and angry, but if you will turn to God, He will lift this burden from you. He will give you the understanding I know you have been searching for. The confusion will leave your mind. You'll make sense of this. The Word of God will open your eyes."

"Beatrice. Thank you for your patience. But I don't want to continue this conversation at this time. If you still wanna watch the child, I'll give him to you tomorrow. I'm not interested in your religion at the moment. I never asked God for anything in my life, so far. After what He's just done, I don't feel He's a God of love. I can't trust Him. I don't need Him. Perhaps, someday, I'll see things differently. Maybe change my mind. But right now, I've made my choice and I'll live with it!"

"Martin." replied Beatrice, "I'm sorry that you feel this way. I don't mean to hurt you or offend you. Because I care, I share the truth with you. In fact, I must share the truth with you. I'll always pray for you and your family. I'll pray for the direction of your in-laws and their provision, which they'll need. I'll be by later to pick up the child. Please call me and let me know about the funeral arrangements for Mary. Yes?"

"Ok." said Martin.

7
BEATRICE AND JAMES

When Beatrice returned to her apartment, she found her husband, James, on his knees in prayer. Beatrice thought about her husband. He was such a great man. No one understood the wonderful work God did in his life. James grew up in the projects in Springfield. His life was full of extreme violence. James was shot and stabbed more than once in his young life. He witnessed his brother die violently in a gang war and his sister die from a drug overdose. His Dad was a violent drunk, who severely beat his wife until James reached young adulthood. James stood over six and a half feet tall and weighed about three hundred pounds. He easily beat a man, who had once terrified his family, into unconsciousness! James became the unchallenged leader of the housing projects. He took vengeance on the drug pusher who sold the poison to his sister. Even the police feared him. Just when it looked as if James would continue in his chosen path of destruction, God showed He had other plans. One day, James was trying to rob an old man. The poor man apparently found himself on the wrong side of town in an area ruled by James and his gang. But an elderly saint of God conquered this vicious, young warrior; who had never lost, who had beaten the toughest opponents the streets had to offer who was known as this "terror of the projects."

33

The elderly saint took James authority away by fearlessly using the name of Jesus against him. He rebuked James to his face using the name of Jesus. This caught James and his gang totally by surprise. They were completely stunned. They repented as this fearless man of God preached the message of salvation and His great love to James and his gang. The man was now finished and these young, supposedly tough gangsters; gave their hearts to the Lord. They gave the elderly man an escort back to his territory in safety. It was shortly after his conversion Beatrice met James at the church she attended. The Pastor had given this young man an opportunity to share his testimony. Beatrice just happened to be there. She was awe struck over his story. James shared how God delivered him. From that moment on, they started dating. Within 6 months, they were married! It was amazing, to Beatrice, to realize they were going on twenty years of marriage.

James carried an awesome testimony. God totally and completely changed a life. James became was a true man of prayer and had profound compassion. It was James who first sensed Mary and her son were in serious danger. James tried to talk to Martin, but he wouldn't listen. Martin saw nothing wrong in Mary's religious beliefs; as long as she kept them to herself and didn't try to convert him. What harm could come from getting together once or twice a month to pray to her god? Didn't all roads lead to heaven? Wasn't it man's privilege to worship God in any way he or she chose? What difference did it make what name you call Him? Martin thought James was just being narrow-minded and bigoted; to think that Jesus was the only way to God.

Mary was completely intimidated by James and would barely say hello to him. Mary told Martin, that whenever James was around, she felt extremely nervous and couldn't help shaking. Martin told her it was because James was so large. Mary replied very strangely to that. She confided it was not so much the outward man who made her afraid, but it was the inner man who caused her to tremble. Martin just chalked it up to Mary's foolish religious beliefs. Sensing Beatrice had come home;

James rose from his knees and embraced his wife. He serenely asked, "How did it go with Martin?"

"Well, Honey," she sighed, "he wouldn't listen, as usual. I've never met a man so stubborn and set in his ways."

"I don't know Beatrice," shared James, in a comforting tone, "but I had the honor of meeting his parents and they are wonderful people. He has surely drifted from their teachings. He's gone his own way. But what's going on with the boy?"

Beatrice replied, "I pick the child up tomorrow when Martin calls. He'll call a little later this afternoon with the funeral arrangements for Mary. It's scheduled for tomorrow morning."

"He did make it clear, that as soon as he puts his life in order, he wants the boy back. People can say what they want about Martin, but he loves his children. James, while we have the boy, we'll bring him to Pastor Strong. I'm going to ask him if he'd pray for him. Wouldn't it be wonderful, if during this time while we have him, he received a miracle and could walk? What would Martin say then? He couldn't really deny that God exists or loves, right?"

"Yes Beatrice," agreed James, "but I feel that we need to pray more than just for his legs. I sense that this child's very life is marked by the enemy and will be a constant struggle. He must be set free. We must pray for this child!"

"Remember, Martin is the covering and authority over him. There isn't much more we can do at this time. Praise God, we can pray for him and love him. These seeds of prayers and love will not come back void. Let's keep that in mind."

8
GOOD - BYE MOM

The next morning came fast. Martin called the night before. He explained the details of Mary's funeral. He'll come by with the boy after the funeral was over. Beatrice and James hurried to prepare the apartment for the boy and get ready for the funeral. They wouldn't attend the reception, just the church ceremony. Both felt they needed to pay their respects to Mary, and her family. The day went as expected. The funeral ceremony wasn't very long, but still; and full of a deep sorrow. All the children were there and looked completely lost. Beatrice and James remained a short distance from the family while the funeral was taking place. They prayed during the mass. They prayed for peace and wisdom for Martin. They prayed for God's perfect will to be accomplished in the decisions Martin would have to make. They also prayed for protection over the children. They wondered what was ahead for them. As soon as the mass was over, they left the church and came back home to wait for Martin to bring the boy.

Shortly after dusk, a knock came at the door. Martin stood, holding his son. Martin also brought his two daughters, as he planned to drop the boy off, first. The girls were going to their uncles' home. Martin didn't have much to say. He wanted to express his appreciation to James and Beatrice for coming to the funeral. He also wanted to thank them for taking his son.

He promised he'd be in touch, soon, to see how his son was doing. He left his brother's phone number in case there were any problems; or if they needed anything. After the girls sadly kissed their brother good-bye, Martin finished his conversation. He excused himself so he could go to his brother's home. Martin pulled up outside his brother's house. Martin and the girls said goodbye. There was so much sadness on their faces. What pain this man was going through; losing his wife at such a young an age. Placing his children with other family members and strangers. Everyone knew how much he loved his family. In spite of all his faults, Martin was a good and faithful father. His world crumbled as his family was torn apart. Beatrice, just before they left, asked Martin for permission to take the boy to church and have them pray for him. Martin said it was OK with him, just as long as they understood that was not his religion. Now, it was time for the boy to get to know them a little before bedtime. The boy was confused and whimpered a bit, but Beatrice prayed for peace. They gave him some milk and cookies. He loved milk and cookies. After he was done, they showed him his room. They got him ready for bed and remained with him until he fell asleep. Morning would be here before he knew it. The next day was Sunday and the service started at 11am.

What a morning it had been. The day started just like any other Sunday; but now a new addition was waiting to be taken care of. Beatrice and James rose early to pray before the boy woke up and breakfast was prepared. When they heard the boy, they got him out of bed. Everyone showered and ate. Dressed for church and off they went. Everything was going great! They entered the parking lot of the church and walked to the front door. Suddenly, the boy started to squirm and fuss. Beatrice held him firmly and sang softly to him, but he wouldn't calm down. His behavior worsened while they were sitting in the pews listening to the Pastor and trying to sing some songs. They were waiting for the Pastor to call them up. The time finally came. The pastor called them up to pray over the boy; but all he could do was scream. What's going on, thought Beatrice? He's acting as if he's being tormented. The Pastor anointed him with oil and the boy immediately lashed out at him. He tried to bite his hand. James had to take the young boy because Beatrice couldn't hold him any longer. The Pastor and the elders of the church looked at the child with shock and confusion. James quietly laid his hand on the child's head. Calmly, but firmly, he rebuked the tormenting spirits, which were troubling him, in the authority of Jesus Christ. Instantly, the boy calmed down and fell quietly asleep in James's arms. The congregation couldn't help but stare. Some looked perplexed; others looked on in absolute amazement. What kind of child is this? Why is this child troubled with spirits? What had his mother exposed him to?

The pastor and the elders dealt with demoniacs before; but never with one so young and so powerful. James actually had to take authority over the situation in Jesus' name. The young child would break into a fit every time a song about the blood of the Lamb was sung or the name of Jesus was mentioned. This child had to be protected and he would be as long as they were with him. The assignment Satan had for him would not be completed. What was to become of him? When was he going to be given back to the family? His mother passed away in the beginning of October. Beatrice and James assumed the boy would be with them until at least January, maybe February. Each day became easier, but they did see behavior, which belied how the enemy would use him. The battle was obvious when he entered the church or if they had friends over; particularly when they had Bible studies at their home. When they had a Bible study, they always opened with a few songs of worship and praise, maybe sharing a grateful testimony of what God had recently done in their lives, and then study of the Word. Martin kept in touch with Beatrice, checking up on the boy and asking how everything was going. Then the Holiday season came.

Martin was really in no mood to have a nice time. But he came to both holidays; picked up the child and went to his brother's house for the family gathering. Every time Martin returned him, he came back happy. That brought joy to Beatrice and

James. The joy radiated from the child's face. So much so that they knew whatever they had been doing was making a difference. The simple love and prayers Beatrice and James poured out of their hearts were chipping away the dark deception. They knew the enemy was bound. They knew the victory belonged to them because of their God. The Word of God says that *His Word will not return to Him void.* The last holiday they shared with him was Christmas. He loved the lights and of course the food. There were special goodies and simple presents. They would play and play.

The time for Martin to take him away was coming, soon. They couldn't bear to see him go. He became a part of Beatrice and James. Yes, they received some looks from people when they saw them all together. Even though they were African American, and the child was white, they knew it was right. Their own church started to have a softer heart towards this relationship, not that they were negative on the whole. Just a few had a hard time with it; because of society's cultural prejudices. But as the Lord stirred their hearts, they finally, little by little, saw their feelings were not in line with the character and heart of God.

Beatrice realized we all have to make the right choices concerning who we are to marry. When God tugs on your heart to do something completely contrary to your own ideas and traditions; your only decision is to give in to God or you'll be missing the mark, so to speak. You'll miss His perfect will for you! Peace will not fully manifest in your heart. Perhaps you won't have any peace at all! Beatrice believed God is a line crosser. Beatrice didn't believe in coincidences. She believed God chooses whom we have fellowship with. Staying among our own sometimes keeps us in traditions, which can never change us from within. Man has a hard time respecting and loving someone else; unless he realizes they are the same as he is in many ways, except for cultural differences. But God offers a supernatural love, which we must first receive, from Him. Then we can share our newfound love with God, with ourselves and with others. If we can't love anyone here on earth with God's love, then you won't love him or her in heaven, because you won't be there. *If the love of God does not abide within you, then you are like a sounding gong.*

Heaven is about love and mercy and forgiveness... righteousness, peace and joy in the Lord.

9
LEAVING THE ARMS OF LOVE

The time came. Martin called a few days ahead. He was coming on Saturday to pick up the boy. Oh God! How are we going to handle this? What about they boy? He went through so much transition after the death of his mother. And then no Dad around! These thoughts concerned Beatrice. Martin arranged to stay with his brother, and his wife. When James and Beatrice heard the news they knew the roller coaster ride was going to begin. The boy was really going to need prayer; now more than ever before! It tore Beatrice and James's heart to know they had to give the child back. They knew Martin loved him, though, and knew he had the boy's best interests were at heart. James asked Martin if he could pray for him and the boy. "The boy yes, me no!" Martin affirmed.

James bowed his head and petitioned God for the safety of the boy; as well as the healing of his legs and voice. "We know some day, in spite of whatever the enemy means for harm, You, God, will restore and more! Someday, he will be a voice for God."

∼ A large shadowy figure appeared ∼

After James lifted up his head from prayer, unnoticed by all, a large shadowy figure appeared in the hallway of the apartment house. Martin was standing at the door. This menacing figure

43

came to express his corrupt and depraved thoughts about the child and his future. Its expression was one of uncontrollable anger and seething hate. This was his son. Who were these insignificant Christians? How dare they stand against him and his will! Did they think they could take this child from him? Did they think they could change any of the curses that were placed on this child by the masters' own desire. What about the curses from the commitment and relationship the mother had with him? These two Christians have power and are hindering his plans for his chosen vessel. They must be stopped!

The master has no power over them. He can only work through weak, willing vessels to attack them. He is subjected to spiritual laws, authority in the name of Jesus and the Blood of the Lamb. On the other hand, men cannot be so easily bound by spiritual laws. They have freewill and so much wonderful liberty to obey, or disobey, by their own choice. Even though the master can't touch one hair on the head of these two, he knows he can use his human slaves to destroy them. It is so easy for the master to turn these silly humans against each other. They love to gossip, slander, and backbite one another. In fact, sometimes it almost seemed unjust to the master. He is always being blamed for strife among these petty creatures; even when he had nothing to do with their rebellious ways. In many of these cases their own flesh, their own lusts and selfish desires are far stronger influences on them than he ever could be. It's a blessing, to use the term lightly. Most of mankind will never learn, in their lifetimes, how truly powerful they are because of the sacrifice of the enemy's Son. The strength of the master rests on deception and the lies. As long as he can keep man in the dark, he will have victory. Most of the time, the master is quite successful in doing this; even among the camp of the enemy.

Occasionally he runs across a couple like James and Beatrice, who arc so aware of the enemy and their position in Christ; that he can't prevail against them. Every time he tried, there was always the power of the Blood and the name of Jesus they believed in. Because of this, he can't touch them. They carry the favor of God. The master and the entire spiritual kingdom are subjected to the Blood, the name, and the Word of God; but humans were a different story. They can be used to destroy even the most righteous of the enemy's followers. All you have to do is add a little jealousy, gossip and bitterness to their pride and even the master is amazed at the amount of division and destruction he can cause in the enemy's ranks. He hopes they'll never learn the secret of unity.

My, what wonderful memories he had of that great tower whose top would reach the heavens; made in that wonderful place called Babel. Babel means Gate of God. His plan would have worked, if the enemy hadn't interfered and caused confusion by changing every one's language. What a mess. Confusion everywhere. No one understood anyone else. Man finally became so confused he gave up the work and abandoned the great tower. The people went their separate ways according to their language. What a lesson to be learned about the power of unity and the tongue. The master also remembered another time of unity not so glorious to him. It was in the upper room, in the city called Jerusalem, where his worst nightmare occurred; oh, how he hated that night. These two events in that city set him back forever. The first was the crucifixion of the enemy's Son. What a horror that turned out to be. If he had only known how that event was going to turnout. He would have left the Christ alone.

The second event was almost as terrible to his kingdom as the first. Somehow, the enemy gathered one hundred and twenty of the followers of His Son in that upper room. They forgot their fears and themselves and came together in unity. God touched the tongues of men and they came together. When they did, *supernatural power came forth as **flaming tongues of fire**!* This Holy Spirit power sent the master and his followers fleeing from the Disciples of Christ. What a difference that power makes in the lives of the believers. Look what happened to his wonderful slave; the one called Saul of Tarsus. He was so trapped in tradition and religion, so filled with bitterness toward the followers of Christ. His puffed up knowledge of

Scripture and his pride caused him to persecute those who
disagreed with him. What wonderful destruction he was doing
to the enemy's camp; until that terrible day on the road to
Damascus.

The master remembered. They were celebrating their victories
over God's people and how much they were looking forward to
the fun they would have in Damascus; until that Light hit Saul
and blinded him. It completely changed him forever; from a
slave of the master, to a loyal servant and faithful apostle of the
enemy. Why even his name was changed from Saul to Paul.
This new creature called Paul, in the end, has done tremendous
damage to his kingdom. He set many free from the clutches of
the master, and in spite of prison and tribulation; he still
managed to write three quarters of the New Testament! 'What
a relief it was when I finally beheaded him. It seems, no matter
how many of the enemy's puppets I destroyed, there are always
others to take their place!' His thoughts returned to these two
spirit-filled saints; James and Beatrice. The master will find a
way and a vessel to get rid of them for what they've done to
this child. "I may not be able to come into their home at this
time, but someday, soon, I'll get even with them!" he
determined in his mind. "This child is my son! He will not be
taken from me or tainted! His supposed father is so easy to use
that my will and assignment must be fulfilled in his life. His
weaknesses will be used for my glory. He will be submissive to
me and do great things for me!"

10
BIG TRANSITION

Martin expressed his gratitude for the care they were giving his son. He picked up the bag containing all the child's belongings as he picked up the child. Martin hated long goodbyes. The child continued to look backwards. He was confused as Martin walked out of the door. He'd call and let them know how everything was going. He was actually saying, Good-Bye. Martin finally settled in his brother's home. The girls and the boy were together again under one roof. Martin worked long hours and was still in transition. It took longer than he'd planned. He thought staying at his brother and his wife's place; was a better choice than being apart any longer. This was going to be another big transition for the boy, but at least they were all together. They were getting used to the neighborhood and their neighbors. Each day the children would play outside. There were lots of dogs, and cats. They were very friendly. Some of them had homes and some were homeless.

One day, while playing outside, a problem arose. The two sisters were struggling to hold their brother down. He was nearly four years old. He was trying to grab at the big man who was holding the stray cat the child had been playing with. This particular cat really loved the child. It would come right up to him whenever he saw him. The animal seemed to sense he

47

couldn't walk.   Since the child couldn't come to him very easily, the cat would go to the child. He would spend hours just letting the child pet him. He was the only friend the child had and now he was in the menacing hands of this large, angry man. The man was yelling at the children. He screamed, "I told you if I ever caught this animal in my garden, I'd kill it. Didn't I?" The girls cried and pleaded, "Please Mr. Silva, the kitty didn't do anything. He was playing with our brother. He's my brothers' only friend. Please don't hurt the kitty!"

"Why should I care about your retard of a brother or this cat?" asked the man. "I warned you children. I told you what would happen if I caught him in the garden."

"I'll tell my Daddy if you hurt the kitty!" the oldest sister threatened.

"Go ahead," said the man, defiantly. "I own this house and if he gives me any trouble, I'll evict him. What'll you do then, you little brats?" The boy tried to break free from his sisters' grip. He even tried to kick the big man, but the man only laughed at the boy's futile efforts.

"Watch this you freaking little punk," said the man. The man bellowed a great roar as he grabbed the animal by the head. With a tremendous twist of his hand, he snapped the cat's neck and threw the dead body at the boys' feet.
Rage burned through the child's heart as he locked eyes with the giant in front of him. With one last surge of strength he flung his sisters backwards and, pointing his finger at the man, spoke his first words. "**DIE!**" cursed the child, "**DIE!**" The man fell clutching his chest. The girls ran screaming for help. The big man lying motionless on the ground was puzzled. He was in great shape. He had no medical problems, yet he couldn't breathe. The pains in his chest were unbearable. The only thing worst than the pain was the look in the eyes of the child standing over him. Somehow, he knew this freak, this retard, was the cause of his pain. The man finally heard a noise and looked up. He saw the boy's father, Martin, pick up his

son and speak to him; trying to calm the child down. As the anger left the child, the pain in the man's chest subsided.

Martin looked him in the eye and spoke. "John, what's going on? The girls told me you killed the cat and then threatened to evict us. John, you don't own this house. My brother does. If you ever bother my children again, I'll not only beat you senseless, I'll have you evicted. Now, one more thing; children go upstairs and don't turn around. John, stand up!" John, still shaking from the intense pain, stood up. As big as he was, he was nowhere near the size of Martin. John tried to take a step backward. Martin grabbed him by the throat. John would have almost welcomed the chest pain back compared to the power he felt in the hands of this man. Martin spoke firmly and directly to John, warning him "If you ever scare my children again, call my son a retard, or belittle him in any way again; I'll hurt you so bad, you'll beg to die! Do you understand me John?" The man fearfully nodded his head and Martin let him go.

When he felt Martin was far enough away to be safe, the man yelled over his shoulder, "He's a freak! He's a freak and should be locked up!" Martin bent down to pick up the dead cat. A figure moved in the shadows behind him. The dark figure smiled a terrible smile. The boy learned a valuable lesson today. He had, for the first time, revealed the power, which lies within him. It is now time to send mentors to train him. As for John, though he is the vessel chosen to teach the child this lesson; he will have to pay for insulting the child. The boy belongs to the master. The master calls him his son. He is his to do with as he pleases; but no one else is allowed to speak against the boy.

A couple of days later, Martin is eating breakfast. His brother walks in with some surprising news. "Good morning, Martin. Did you hear what happened to John last night?"

"No," Martin replied. "What?"

"Well it seems he stopped to fix a flat tire on his way home from work. He collapsed on the side of the road. By the time they got him to the emergency room, he was dead. It's so strange. John wasn't the brightest person we know, but he did keep himself in good shape. Something else is really weird. The doctor told his wife it looked like a giant hand had crushed his heart? It was so terribly misshapen."

"Well Don," said Martin, "you know John ate a lot of junk. And the other day, when he was yelling at the kids, the girls told me he collapsed with pain in his chest. It may have been a warning. He should've had it checked out. What's his wife going to do?"

Martin's brother replied, "Well, John was an idiot. But his wife has always been pleasant and helpful to Susan. I'll let her live here 'rent free' for a few months until she gets back on her feet."

Martin offered, "If there's anything else I can do to help her, Don, let me know. I know how it feels to lose a loved one. At least there are no children involved."

"Speaking of the children, Martin; how's your son handling the loss of that stray?"

"He took it real hard," replied Martin. "The girls told me he even yelled at John to die. This will truly shake him up when he finds out John died." Later that night, when Martin told the children what happened, the girls cried and asked their father, "Will the boy be put in jail for telling John to die?" Martin told them no. He had nothing to do with the death of John. It was just a coincidence. He explained this in detail to his daughters, so they could receive peace of mind.

The boy just sat, staring. Although he couldn't talk, he could hear. He was listening to a voice speaking to him, telling him he has the power to punish anyone who would hurt him or those he loved. Maybe his father doesn't believe, but the boy

50

knows. Didn't the voice tell him help was being sent to teach him how to use his power? The voice also shared with him that things were going to change during the stay at Aunt Susan's house."

The next day came; bringing with it ominous storm clouds by evening. Heavy rains began to fall a little later. The lightning flashed and the thunder shook the house. All the lights had gone out. Aunt Susan lit the candles and gathered all the children in the living room to pray to the Virgin Mother; so the sailors at sea would be protected. The boy refused, again! Aunt Susan was astounded and still couldn't believe this child would say no, especially to her and her ways. The child had crossed his aunt. She was angrily yelling at him, telling him he was a bad seed. The 'Diablo' was waiting in his bedroom under his bed; to drag him to hell when he fell asleep. This behavior was nothing unusual for Aunt Susan.

Every time a thunderstorm came, she would gather all the children in the living room to pray. The boy would always refuse. He didn't know any sailors and he thought it was too much effort to talk. He was going on five years old and could now walk. But it was very difficult for him to speak. There was no way he was going to waste effort on sailors whom he didn't know. Once, when the boy did ask his aunt why she liked sailors so much, she became enraged and threatened him with damnation. After a good half hour or so, she'd send him to his room and returned to praying with the rest of the children. The boy cried. It seemed every adult thought it their job to beat him and tell him how stupid and useless he was; everyone but his grandfather.

Martin's father came over from time to time. He was the only man who was an example of gentleness and compassion to the boy. He was a ray of sunshine in the boy's life. When he was with his grandfather his handicap didn't matter. The kind man treated him with love and kindness. He always showed him so much attention. He loved the long walks he always took with his grandfather. It was wonderful. This good man knew all about flowers and plants. He knew which ones could be used for healing and which ones made great teas. The only time the boy smiled was when he was with his grandfather. His grandparents would read to him from a big black Book of wonderful stories. The boy loved the stories. Many times he felt afraid, though. He heard voices telling him not to listen to those stories. He'll be punished for doing so. When he stayed at his grandparents' place, each night his grandmother would make him pray. But not like his aunt; who always prayed to the Virgin or to some saint. His grandmother would make him pray directly to God, the Father, in Jesus' name. The voices became very fearful when his grandmother or grandfather prayed. When his grandfather prayed, the voices would try to make the boy act in violent ways to make them stop. It was amazing to the boy that when his Aunt Susan prayed to the Saints or to the Virgin; the voices never reacted in a negative way. They seemed to draw strength from her prayers. There was no big black book in her house. Her priest told her she couldn't understand it without their help. She was always going to the priest to talk with him or to confess something.

11
ATTEMPTED EXORCISM

The transition for the boy at his aunt's house was to be a hard one. One thing would lead to another and he would inevitably find himself in trouble. Every time Aunt Susan had a problem, especially with the boy, she'd call her priest. One particular day she brought the boy to him. This was just one of the many times; but now she was fed up. While in one of their sessions, the priest made a comment that offended the boy. He believed the boy's grandparents were going to hell because they were not a member of his religion. As soon as the boy heard this, his eyes glared at the priest with intense anger. The priest was holding a pair of beads. When the priest shared his belief about the boy's grandparents, the beads exploded and the priest fell backwards. He recovered and warned the boy's aunt. He told her the boy was no good and needed to be punished. The session ended. The boy knew she was upset. "Oh no!" said the boy, "I'm in trouble again. But no one talks about my grandparents that way, not even the priest!"

As soon as she walked in her house she slapped the boy across the face. She immediately began screaming and calling him a bad seed and sent him to his room. Later, that night the priest came by. The boy's father and uncle wouldn't be home for a few days. It was funny; the priest never came when the men were home. He came that night for a few hours, though. They went behind closed doors and talked. The door opened. The boy's aunt made him come into the room and sit in a chair. She tied his hands and legs. The aunt had her son and his sisters kneel and pray to the Virgin and St. Michael the archangel. She prayed they'd come and punish the boy until the Diablo left him. The priest grabbed his holy water and sprinkled it on the boy's head. He prayed long prayers in a strange language. Everything seemed to be going well until the boy spoke to the priest in that very same strange language. The priest became pale and began to tremble. The priest told the boy's aunt what he said. She became afraid. How did he know what was going on behind closed doors? God forbid, if her husband found out. He would never understand. He was not spiritual, as she was. The priest once again tried to muster up enough courage to approach the boy. Once more he sprinkled him with holy water and commanded the spirits to leave. The voices in the boy just laughed as if they were enjoying a private joke. The more the priest prayed the more the boy laughed.

The boy once again spoke in that same strange language. The boy finally noticed something; when his grandparents prayed or Beatrice and James prayed, they used the enemy's name. They prayed with authority, which quieted the voices. When the priest prayed and performed his rituals, he said this "in the name of the Father, the Son and the Holy Ghost;" without using the enemy's name. The voices then began to come alive. Many times he wouldn't use those titles but made his petitions in the name of the Virgin. ***Now the boy was wondering about the difference in the forms of prayers and how the voices reacted.***

The objects in front of him began to move across the room. First, it was pencils, then dishes, and finally the chair the boy was sitting in. The aunt and the priest grew very, very nervous. They realized this was beyond their understanding and ability. She began to yell, hysterically, at the children. Pray more! Pray more! She demanded they pray more to Saint Jude. Two hours of prayer tediously passed while the holy water was sprinkled on him. The boy finally looked at the priest and smiled; and with great effort stated, "Thank you father. You have shown me the error of my ways. I thank you, the virgin, and saints. And let's not forget my aunt for showing me the path I am to walk."

The relieved priest replied, "May the Virgin bless you!" He nodded his head and smiled with approval. His aunt broke down and cried. She told the children to stop praying and untie him. His aunt made a big meal. After everyone had eaten their full, she sent the children to bed. The priest and Aunt Susan sat in the living room, again behind closed doors. They didn't notice the boy was up and listening at the door. When the priest began to stand up the boy scooted around the door to peek. He saw them hug. The priest left and drove off. The boy smiled for the voices were speaking once again to him. They were telling him how easy it was to deceive these religious fools at their own game. They don't know how to test the voices to see if it is truly God or not.

Later, that night, as the boy was preparing himself for bed, he became aware of a large spirit standing in the corner of his room. This didn't surprise the boy. He'd noticed spirits before, not as large as this one, but he was used to seeing them. This spirit approached the boy and began to speak to him. The shadowy specter warned the boy, he would personally destroy him if he tried to disobey the master at anytime. As long as he walked in strict obedience to the Dark Lord; he and others at his command would be there to serve him, use their power on his behalf, and even loan their power to him! The spirit told the boy the master was pleased with him. He was pleased with the charade the boy played on the priest and his aunt. The boy was given one more warning of destruction; if he should ever disobey…then the spirit vanished!

The boy lay awake a long time wondering what was happening in his life. Surely he wasn't normal. His sisters didn't see and talk to spirits; or hear voices! They couldn't move objects with their minds. They could never feel the power flow from their bodies as he did. Why was he so different? Was he truly a bad seed, something evil from birth, as his aunt said? The boy learned his lessons well. Whenever the priest would come to visit he would disappear; otherwise he would be polite and obedient. He would pretend he was interested in what the priest had to say. Once the boy would question the priest, anger would arise. The boy would find himself locked in his room for two whole days. He simply asked the priest. "If you believed in God so much, why don't I ever see you reading the Bible like my grandmother? Do you believe in a different God?

than she does?" When he promised he'd never ask another question like that again and apologized for his rudeness, his aunt allowed him to come out of his room. The boy learned how to avoid future problems by playing the game the way the master had shown him. The master seemed to receive great pleasure watching his aunt in her religious activities. He seemed to encourage her to pray to the saints and to make novenas.

It appeared to the boy that all religions seem to flow directly to the master. He gained more and more strength from their various forms of worship. In one of his training sessions, the boy's mentor told him all religions except for the fanatical Christian, belong to the master. Even though all these religions served the master to varying degrees; there was a difference between the teachings of these other groups and what the boy was being taught. These other 'religions' blindly serve the master whom they don't really know. But the boy and his teachers have the great honor to know the master and serve him directly!

12
SEASON OF PEACE

The boy's dad told him a change was coming again. He was happy with the news. He didn't have to be tied up any longer or called a bad seed. He was moving in with his grandparents for a little while. His father told him to gather his things together today. They will leave tomorrow morning. The boy was extremely happy, crying out loud, "OH BOY! Treats and all! I'll even have nice long walks with Grandpa again. He shows me so much! All about flowers and what kind they are. He takes me to the store and buys me candy and ice cream." Then the boy thought to himself, "Maybe I won't feel so bad and hate myself so much now. I don't know how much more I can take. No one accepts me for me. No one cuddles me and hugs me and tells me how good I am. I wonder why I'm leaving? Why aren't the girls going, too? Who cares? I'm leaving."

The day went by as any other day; except he was collecting his modest belongings in a box, as dad asked him to. It was almost time for dinner. Shortly after dinner it was tub time; and then to bed. After the boy was settled into bed, the master appeared. He warned the boy that he'd know everything the boy did. The boy was never to become involved with his grandmother's church. He could continue to go to his aunt's church and follow the religion of the priest but at no time should he ever embrace the teachings of his grandmother. The master warned him that if he did, he'd destroy the boy's grandparents. The boy promised not to betray the master. Still, his young mind saw no difference in the churches. They were all weak, though the voices would listen better with grandmother's religion. They had no real power like the master had. He did discover many of the master's followers attended these churches; and many were in leadership positions! Although the boy still had difficulty speaking and walking, he wasn't stupid. He knew this spiritual power developing inside him could easily be taken away from him and given to another. Even at this young age the boy understood power. He knew he was bound by his word. Once he gave his word to anyone he would not break it. He learned that a promise is an oath. It is not to be taken lightly. This was an important lesson of obedience and submission, which had to learn. Keeping your word and especially your promises eventually resulted in more power and more gifts. He promised his master he would be faithful. *The power of life and death is in the tongue!*

If there were another God, where was he? If he was so strong and had so much power, then why was the boy handicapped? What horrible deed had been done against this so-called God that would justify crippling him? He didn't know whom else to blame it on. On the other hand, the master promised, that at the proper time, he would heal him. But the boy will have to prove his loyalty. He understood nothing was freely given. You had to earn all things. The master was absolutely pleased with the boy's attitude and his willingness to humble himself before the master. They had to admit the boy was showing great progress and loyalty. In spite of the handicaps, the power was growing. The boy's soul was being opened to allow the dark spirits of the masters to enter him. Already the overlord Shiva, who the Hindus called the Destroyer, started to set up camp in the boy. The boy now fell asleep to wake up to a new day and his grandparents! He was so excited.

Morning came. They gathered around the table for breakfast. Everything went fine, but the boy kept feeling a new change was coming. Dad was beginning to be happy again. He was getting to be more like he used to be; before he lost Mary. The move to his grandparents went smoothly. The boy had a hard time making friends with the neighborhood children, though, because of his inability to speak. But his fists earned him a position in the group, eventually. He beat the local bully and his brother at the same time! The other children decided it was better to have him on their side, instead of on the bully's side. The boy didn't really care why they wanted to be his friend. He just wanted friends. It was getting harder and harder to relate to others since he was unable to express himself verbally. Soon he'd be going to school like his sisters. They told him he'd need to talk clearly or the kids would all make fun of him. He didn't want that. He had enough pain in his young life. Right now he was trying to be happy with where he was and whom he was with. He just wanted to enjoy everyday he had with them.

Every afternoon the boy and his grandfather would go for long walks. His grandfather would try to help him speak more clearly. He loved this wonderful man. The boy felt so safe with him. It seemed that even the master feared to come near the boy when his grandfather was around. There was a quiet strength about him. It seemed to fill him from within.

His dad wasn't like Grandfather. Martin had no sense of strength in this way. Grandfather never yelled or beat him. He was always patient and gave the boy all the time he needed to answer or explain himself. The boy never paid attention to his handicap while he was with his grandfather. Life was really good now. His dad was working and every weekend he would see his sisters. They'd all have pizza together and see a movie. Things couldn't be much better than this!

13
MEET DEBRA!

One particular weekend arrived. The boy's father had some news for the children. It seemed they were about to have a new addition to the family. This will bring a whole new path again into their lives. New changes will be made. They're going to have a new mother! Each child will spend a weekend with her, so they can get to know her. The oldest sister will go first and then the younger sister; then finally, the boy. The boy remembered how he felt about his Dad before he left his uncle's house. He saw the change in his Dad and how happy he seemed to look. Now he knew why. The day arrived and it was his oldest sister's turn to visit with dad's new love. The weekend seemed to go by fast and she couldn't wait to share her weekend with her sister and the boy. She had wonderful stories to share of her visit. She spoke affectionately of the lady and how nice she was. She shared the fun things they did together. She displayed the toys she was given. His sister told him about the lady's dog and what a good cook she was. The boy couldn't wait for his turn.

The next weekend, the other sister spent the weekend with the lady. Her name was Debra. She too, had a great weekend, just like her older sister. She returned with her presents and wonderful stories. The boy waited all week for his turn. There was so much expectancy. What a wonderful time he was going to have. Maybe a peace and goodness was going to come and remain in the family. The weekend finally came. He was still having a hard time saying Debra. She came to pick him up at his grandparent's home. She talked with his grandfather about the boy. He invited her to have lunch with him, his wife and grandson. Debra accepted the offer. After lunch they walked to the bus stop together and took the bus to the lady's house. The boy was amazed she lived only a few blocks away from his grandparents. On the bus, the lady explained how she met his father on the job. They'd be married in a couple of weeks. She also revealed they would come to live with her. The boy asked her if she really had a dog and she told him yes. She had a dog and he could play with him! It seemed to take forever to arrive home. The boy couldn't wait. Finally, this was his weekend to have fun, just as his sisters had! He could hardly believe he'd have two parents living in the same house again! Finally, it was going to be his turn to brag about his adventures to his sisters and show off his gifts. The bus stopped at the top of the hill and it took him just a few minutes to walk to her house. The lady's home was cute with a nice yard. There was a basketball hoop in the backyard, which belonged to the teenage boy who lived in the house behind Debra. As they entered the house; Debra told the boy to go into the bathroom and fill the sink with water. The boy, who wanted to please the lady, quickly filled the sink. His heart was filled with joy. They'd have a mother just like all the other children. They'd all be a family!

The boy was daydreaming as he watched the sink fill up with water. The water reached about three quarters full when he felt something grab his hair on the back of his head and push his face into the water. The boy immediately started to panic. He couldn't breathe! He was dizzy. Just as he was losing consciousness his head was yanked out of the water and he could finally breathe. After a moment, he was thrust underwater again. He was terrified and felt helpless! This happened two or three times. Finally, the last time the boy passed out. He woke up on the floor of the bathroom. Debra was standing over him. She was no longer pretty and her face was full of rage and hate. Her words cut the boy's heart. She screamed at him. "Welcome to hell, you little retard! Your nightmare has only just begun. You'd better do everything I tell you, when I tell you or you'll pay the price!" After making the boy clean up the water and dry himself off, she took him and locked him in a closet. She told him this was his bedroom until he learned to obey her in all things. During the whole weekend the boy was only allowed out of the closet to use the bathroom. Although the weekend went by quickly; which was a blessing to the boy, it was unforgettable. He was terrified.

While the boy was on his way home; he was warned to never tell what happened. If he revealed anything, he wouldn't be allowed to live with his father and sisters! She threatened to take them far away where he'd never see them again. She also told him she knew all about the master and his plans for the boy's life. She'd tell them the boy wasn't willing to obey the master any longer. Debra so terrified the boy he promised he wouldn't say a thing.

When he finally arrived home, he told everyone he had a good time. The sisters asked about the bruise on his forehead. He continued lying and said it happened while playing. His sisters asked him why he didn't have any gifts. He simply said the lady was too busy to go shopping. The young boy's heart was broken. He couldn't tell anyone why; not even his beloved grandfather. Everyone seemed to really like the lady, especially his grandfather. She was always nice to him. The only one who didn't appear to be taken in by her was grandmother. She wasn't completely in favor of this marriage; but, still, she didn't believe the boy's story. She accused him of making up tales to keep his Dad from getting married. The week went by awfully fast and before he knew it, another weekend was upon them. This was the last weekend with his grandparents. He was going to cherish this last remaining time. One more week and his dad would be married. Oh my God, a perfect life was coming to an end! What was going to happen now?

Saturday came. The wedding began at two o'clock. It was a simple wedding. During the ceremony, all the boy could hear, over and over again in his mind, were her threatening words.

"Welcome to hell you little retard. From this moment on your life belongs to me; to do with as I please. Remember, if you tell anyone I'll take your father away, forever!" The marriage ceremony concluded. After the ceremony the couple went away for a few days on their honeymoon. The boy still had some time with his grandparents. He was trying to push away the sadness growing in his heart. Now, when he finally had some happiness in his life; it was taken away! The move to Debra's house went without any problems. A few weeks passed and everyone seemed happy. Dad would come home nightly from work. It actually felt like one big happy family.

One night, about a month after the boy and his family moved in to Debra's house, the boy experienced a horrifying nightmare. The master appeared to him in a grotesque and terrifying form. In the dream, he showed the boy a vision straight from hell! The boy saw people tormented in many ways. The master brought the boy's attention to a wretched young woman. She seemed to be the object of the full measure of the master's wrath. The boy was told this was his real mother. Because the boy wasn't learning fast enough, she was being punished for his failures. Her torment would only increase if the boy didn't completely obey the master in all things. The boy cried out to the master. "What am I doing so wrong? I told no one about you. I've tried to obey you in all things. I didn't even go to church with my grandparents because you told me not to. Whatever you tell me, I will obey. If you tell me to do something, I will try my best to do it. If you tell me not to do something, I won't do it. There is no need to continue to hurt my mother. **I AM YOURS!**"

∼ Conditioning and training will begin ∼

"We will see," said the master. "In a few more days your *conditioning and training will begin.* Your stepmother will be my tool. Her hands will teach you to obey me in all things. You will put me first. Not even your precious grandfather will be before me. Your life is mine. I will have my way! No matter what! Do you understand?" screamed the master.

"Yes master." replied the boy, as he slowly slipped to his knees in front of him. ***"I bow to you from a willing heart, for there is none like you.*** Please don't let my mother suffer. Wasn't she faithful to you, sir? Did she not offer me to you before my birth, as the elders had told me? I don't seek to anger you, master. I accept your will and your ways. Only your will truly matters to me. I'm only asking mercy be shown to one of your faithful ones." The master vanished before the boy woke up, laughing, saying, "Mercy! What Mercy? Mercy is weak and I am not weak! No one tells me when to have mercy! Not even you. You are to become my chosen vessel, is that clear?"

The boy cried again, "Whatever you want I will do!" The voice replied, "We shall see."

14
SCHOOL BEGINS

The boy finally started school. He entered kindergarten. Everyone was amazed. He was excelling, though his speech was not clear. He was a very advanced reader. His handicap kept him from excelling to a higher grade. The boy made friends in school. His friends, and happiness with them, outweighed the unhappy home life of daily beatings and discouragement from Debra. His best friends were Peter and Kenny. They tried to help him with his speech impediment. He made the bullies in the school leave his friends alone. Peter and Kenny told him of a holiday coming up; which everyone participated in. It was called **Halloween**. Peter and Kenny told him all about the holiday and the good things it had to offer. The boy was so excited to participate and receive all the candy he could. His friends taught him how to trick or treat. They would spend time telling him about dressing up in costumes and going door to door for treats. Peter was going to be a cowboy. Kenny wanted to go as Buck Rogers, space hero. The boy just finished reading Treasure Island and he wanted to go as a pirate. His dream, when he became old enough, would be to run away and become one. No one would dare make fun of him because he would make him walk the plank. The more they talked about Halloween, the more excited the boy became. He couldn't wait for that time to come. The elders were also telling the boy about Halloween but they called it by another

67

name. ***They called it San-hein, the night of the dead***.
They encouraged the boy to celebrate this night.

Finally the big day came, and he couldn't wait for the night to
come. The boy's stepmother was talking to his sister when he
got home. Both girls were so excited. The older sister was in a
beautiful princess dress; which Debra made for her. His other
sister was dressed up as a prima ballerina. Their outfits were
beautiful. Debra was really good at sewing. The boy couldn't
wait to see his costume. He dashed into his room. On his bed
were one of his older sister's dresses and some hair ribbon. The
boy came out of his room and asked where his pirate costume
was. After making fun of his speech, his stepmother told him
he was going out as a girl. The boy became so angry. He tried
to yell at her. He tried to tell her he wasn't going out as a girl,
but as a pirate!

Debra became enraged. Her temper flared and she struck the
boy full force across the face! She began screaming, "Do as
you're told or you will pay the price for disobedience!" The
boy tried to stand his ground. "I will not go out as a girl!" He
was going out as a pirate! 'This was the last straw.' she
thought. 'Who did this crippled little retard think he was to talk
back to her? This is my house. Not his. I don't even want him
here. I'm married to his father and I have to let him stay. But I
sure don't have to take any back talk from some retarded freak
like him!'

The boy had no idea how long the beating lasted, but when he
woke up he was in the closet. The door was locked. He knew
not to make any noise because Debra would only become
angry and the boy would pay the price. The boy would just
have to wait it out. His father would come home. Debra always
made sure the boy was back in his room before his Dad came
home. She always had a story to tell his father. How the boy
misbehaved and had to be sent to his room. The boy's father
always made him apologize to Debra. In many cases, he gave
the boy a beating for disobeying as well. The boy knew his

father loved him anyway, even though he never said it. Sitting
perfectly still in the closet, the boy prayed to the master for
help. He had embraced Halloween and he'd been unjustly
punished! Would the master help? The answer was no! The
boy must learn to solve his own problems. Life was unfair.
Only the strong had the right to rule. The weak must to learn
their place through trials and suffering. They are only worthy to
be slaves. If the boy wanted revenge, he'd have to grow strong
and take it himself or remain a weakling and endure the
penalty.

Finally, after what seemed like forever, the closet door was
opened. The boy was roughly pulled out. He had a hard time
opening up his eyes. The first thing he saw was Debra's angry
face. She began to yell at him, "Your father will be home later.
You'd best keep your mouth shut about what happened to you
these last couple of days. Now go and put your clothes on. Get
ready for school."

The boy didn't realize he was in the closet all night and it was
time for school again. "Get ready for school, Junior!" she
yelled again. The boy was confused. What did she mean by the
last couple of days? Had he really been locked up that long?
When he went to his room, he couldn't believe it. There on his
bed was the dress he was supposed to wear trick or treating!
The boy became angry and was about to rush out of the room
to confront Debra, when his older sister suddenly grabbed him.
She shook him. She cried out. "Do what you're told, Butch, or
she'll really hurt you! You've been in the closet for two days.
If I hadn't told her daddy was coming home today, she
wouldn't have let you out. Don't say a word. Sis has already
gone ahead. She'll meet us in the alley behind Armand's with
your clothes."

**His sister called him by his nickname, Butch! He
couldn't believe the name came out of her mouth. He
despised that name.** No one mentioned, let alone called him
by his nickname; except his father. **His father took the name**

69

from his stepmother's dog. In fact, later his stepmother told him that since his nickname was the same as her dog, he wasn't allowed to be called that name ever again! She told him he was lower than the dog. He wasn't worthy of that name. He'd be called Junior; by her and everyone else. Only she'd understand the real meaning. It meant he wasn't even as valuable as the dog. He was just a worthless second-class animal. So when his sister called him by his nickname, he knew she was serious. If Debra had heard her, even though she was Debra's favorite, she'd have been punished.

The boy put the dress on as he was told. He showed himself to his stepmother. The woman handed the boy a sign to wear around his neck. It read, "I AM A SISSY!" Debra glared at him as he left for school. She stared out the window until she couldn't see him any longer. The boy continued to walk. When he knew she couldn't see him, he dashed down the alley where his sisters were waiting. He quickly changed his clothes, but his sisters convinced him to wear the sign. Wearing that sign literally saved him from another beating. When the boy entered the school the teacher couldn't believe what was around his neck. She quickly responded by writing the letter making her point and expressing her disagreement with this example. She felt that although the boy was mentally handicapped, as evidenced by his poor speech; it was a cruel and unnecessary punishment. He was shamed and embarrassed, in spite of his apparent limited understanding.

The children were relieved their plan had succeeded. The boy was deeply disturbed, though, that in spite of his good grades, even his teacher thought he was retarded; just because of his speech problem! The boy learned to be invisible. He'd sit for hours in his room reading. He wouldn't talk to anyone at home, unless they spoke to him, which was very rare. No matter what the boy did, his stepmother would find a reason to punish him. One day, as she was ironing some of his dad's shirts, she called him over and said, "This is an iron." She asked him, "Do you know what this is Junior? It's very hot! Do you understand?"

"Yes." replied the boy. Debra ignored his answer.

She grabbed him by his arm and told him, "Retards don't understand by explanation. They only understand by a demonstration!" She pressed the iron to his hand. The pain was incredible but the boy was determined not to let her see him cry. She released his hand. For the first time the boy saw fear in her eyes. He wouldn't look away from her. She began to tremble and shake. She yelled at him, "Go to go to your room and stay there! There won't be any supper because of your attitude." She thought to herself, 'Here she was trying to teach him an important life lesson and he was giving her an attitude. He acted as if she had done something wrong! Well, he could just stay in his room until he learned to be more appreciative.'

15
THE LESSON

The boy sat in his room, disgusted and confused. He was angry and hurt. At that very moment his spirit guide came to visit him. He began to yell at his guide, "How could you have let this happen? Why didn't you help me?"

The guide just slowly smiled and calmly replied, "It is not my responsibility to teach you to survive. It is yours to learn how. There was *one* thing you did well today. You learned to not let your emotions control you. In the future it will serve you well. You'll learn to not show any emotions or feelings at all! Remember you must bring glory to the master in all things. The master knows he will be able to trust you, no matter what. Your hand will heal and the scar will fade. But, do not let the lesson you learned today ever fade. Remember, people can only do to you what you let them. Only you are responsible for your destiny. Never let your feelings control you. Rather, you remain in control of them throughout all things."

Hours after his guide vanished; the boy was still going over what he was told. He promised himself his stepmother would never see him cry, though. Debra finally came to bandage his hand before his father came home. He said nothing to her. She was so unnerved by his lack of response; she repeatedly slapped him across his face. Finally, when her temper was spent, she just yelled at him. She told him he was worse than a savage beast and should be locked up in a cage away from normal people; before he hurt someone. She stated, "I just don't understand why your father can't see you're just a retarded, useless animal! You should be locked up for your own good, among your own kind. Your mother was the lucky one. She died and didn't have to put up with you!" Debra turned to leave the room. On the way out, she warned the boy, "You better not say anything to your father about what happened today; or I promise you'll brutally pay!" Later that night, the boy heard his stepmother tell his father how he received his injuries.

"I don't know what to do with him." Martin said.

Martin had noticed the boy's face was all bruised. Debra told him it was from fighting in school. "The teachers say he picks fights with other children all the time." said Debra. "I tried to talk to him today. He grabbed the hot iron from me and tried to throw it at me. Martin, he resent me! He seems to hate me so much; no matter how much love I try to show him. Now, he refuses to talk to me or even look at me! He hides in his room for hours pretending he can read! Martin, you know it's impossible for him to read. He can't even speak clearly! Oh, Martin, what can I do to reach this boy? You see how well your daughters and I get along? Is it me, Martin? You know I love you and the children. Please tell me how I can reach the boy."
"Debra, don't worry. You're doing a great job. I know it's hard for you. I work two jobs and you have to spend so much time alone with the children. Don't worry. I will talk to the boy. If I have to, I'll arrange for him to see a doctor for counseling. If they feel he should be locked up, then we'll follow their advice. Now, let me go and talk to him."

As the boy's father came into the room, the boy made up his mind. Two could play this lying game. He knew his stepmother had totally convinced his father it was all his fault and she had done everything she could to show him love. He knew it would take too long to tell his side of the story. Anyway, his father would never believe him. Martin opened the door to his room and called his name. The boy made up his mind. He knew what to do. Martin began to question him. The boy started to cry. "I am a bad boy, Daddy. I do bad things because I'm stupid. I'm not like normal boys. I'm just no good. Debra is so good. She works so hard. I tried to help her with the iron today. Stupid me! I grabbed the hot iron. I didn't know. Not smart like Debra. Burn hand bad. I'm so sorry. I will try hard to be good. I want to help. I just stay in the room by myself. I try to please Debra by reading. I try to make her happy. Debra's love and kindness is nice to me. I'll try to be a better boy. I want her to know I'm good. She makes me feel special to be named after her dog. I'd like to give her a hug and say thank you. Can I?"

Martin replied, "Yes, of course you can." Martin called for Debra.

Debra came in the room. The boy ran to her and hugged her tightly. "Debra!" he cried, "I thank you for your love." Debra cringed as the boy called her by her name. She told him he was never to call her by that name. But, what could she do with Martin sitting there watching it? He continued with this act of gratitude in front of his dad. "Thank you, mother, for this soup I had for supper".

His father corrected him and explained, "We didn't have soup. We had meatloaf."

"Oh?" replied the boy, "It's been so long since I ate. I forgot."

"Are you hungry?" asked his Dad. "There's plenty left over. I'm sure Debra wouldn't mind warming some up for you." The boy could feel her tense up as his father spoke to her. He could sense her anger. He knew someday, he'd pay for this victory; but he didn't care. He'd enjoy his reward for now. Somewhere in the back of his mind the boy could hear his guide laughing. He learned a good lesson. He should always remember the power in words he learned this day. Time went by as normal for the boy. When his father wasn't home, he spent more time in the closet than in his room.

One time he actually went for two weeks without food, because he tried to defend his sister from Debra. Debra forced his sister to eat her own waste because she had an accident in her pants on the way home from school. It was all the boy could take when he saw Debra smear that waste on his sister's face. He lost control and began to hit and kick her. Debra beat him senseless with a stick and then locked him in the closet. It was okay though. He won another small victory. She stopped tormenting his sister.

16
COUNSELOR

Debra's luck seemed to be running out. The wonderful loving mother masquerade was failing and falling apart. Each time his dad returned home, the boy would play a game and win his sympathy. The girls would never tell their father. Perhaps they feared that if they did, Debra would direct her anger at them. This time Debra overstepped her limits with the girls, though. She not only tortured their brother but also directed her temper at one of them. They didn't feel safe anymore.

When the opportunity came, they squealed to their father and told him what happened to Candy. When confronted by Martin, Debra tried to play the incident down. Attributing it to the over active imagination of the children. She told Martin she simply tried to make Candy look at the mess and tell her she was too old for that kind of behavior. Martin wasn't buying the line. He told her if she ever touched his daughters again, he wouldn't hesitate to divorce her. This terrified Debra. As sick as she was, she truly loved Martin and didn't want to leave him. She apologized to Candy and asked for her forgiveness. She never touched the girls again while they remained in the house. She just redirected her anger at the boy. The boy didn't care. It was well worth the price he paid to see his father put Debra in her place.

Hopefully, one day, his Dad will know the truth and will do the same for him, as he had done for his sisters.

～ The worst time of the year was the Holidays ～

Time passed slowly for the boy. Most days and nights were bearable. The worst times of the year were the Holidays. Debra always found a way to ruin them for the boy. On **Halloween,** he always ended up locked in the closet and was never allowed to go out. Thanksgiving, he found the price he had to pay for the meal wasn't worth it. On Easter, his stepmother tried to force the boy to eat a chocolate crucifix. She knew he was in awe of the crucifix. God forbid, if he ever ate the candy given to him. He definitely would pay for that mistake. As far as Christmas was concerned, it was the worst. One Christmas Eve, the boy began to watch the debut of Rudolf the Red-Nose Reindeer. Suddenly, Debra ordered the boy to get up and take the garbage out. The boy went to put his shoes and pants on. Debra flew into a rage screaming, "Did I tell you to put clothes on, Junior?"

"No." responded the boy. "But it's cold outside and there's snow on the ground."

"I don't care!" said Debra. "Take the trash out right now! Just the way you are."

The boy did as he was told. She closed the door behind him and left him outside for three hours. A neighbor called Debra. She threatened to call the police if Debra didn't let him in. Debra resentfully told the elderly woman to mind her own business. The boy was hers to do with as she pleased. If she chose this method to teach her stepson to obey, it was her choice. No one had a say in the matter. Minutes before his Dad came home, Debra let the boy in. She gave him the same line; "Don't tell your Dad!" She told him, "If the incident is brought up; explain that you locked yourself out by mistake. If that nosy neighbor says anything, tell your father the old woman must be mistaken about the length of time you were outside."

His father came home. The incident was never brought up. Even though the neighbor stopped to talk to Martin before he entered the house. Debra even wondered why she didn't say anything. It was the old lady's moment to spill the beans but she didn't. Martin never said a word. Debra assumed the neighbor hadn't mentioned the incident. But Martin felt it was Debra's responsibility to discipline the children, as she felt necessary. It was, generally, her choice of methods to discipline in any way she felt necessary. Besides, Martin wanted to settle in early because it was Christmas Eve. Debra made a lot of goodies to munch on. The tree was decorated and so were the windows. All the presents were wrapped. The children ate a few snacks and went to bed early anticipating Santa's arrival.

Christmas morning finally came. There were gifts for everyone. The sweet aroma of Christmas breads filled the home. Everyone sat down to eat breakfast before opening any gifts. The children enjoyed unwrapping their brightly colored presents. As soon as everything was opened, his sisters put their gifts away. Debra took the boy's gifts and did what she did every year. Hid them! It became a routine. It reached the point where the boy didn't even bother to get up early. He was forced to, though. One Christmas he simply took the gifts that was still wrapped and gave them to Debra. The boy's behavior was rewarded with a serious beating at the hands of this father. Martin couldn't understand why the boy treated Debra that way. Martin thought the boy was unappreciative. He called the boy a spoiled brat. Martin told him he didn't deserve his stepmother's kindness and love.

Something snapped in the boy's heart that day. He no longer cared, nor feared, what could be done to him. His spirit was broken. He'd been beaten, burned, and locked in his closet. Repeatedly! He went without food for days on end. His head was split open on three separate occasions; once with a butcher knife, once with a frying pan, and once with a glass bottle. When his legs began to turn in, because of the effects of the meningitis; instead of going to the doctor, his stepmother simply turned his legs outward and tied them to the bed. What more could be done? There were simply no more feelings left in the boy. He no longer cared if his father loved him or not. This day, which was supposed to be a Christian holiday, turned into a nightmare from someone he loved the most! Here he was, on Christmas morning, lying in his own blood! The boy cried out in pain and defiance, *"I don't care anymore!* Beat me all you want. Starve me! Lock me up and deny it. There's nothing you can do to hurt me any more. My mother is dead! Debra will never be my mother!" The boy crawled to his room. He closed the door and wouldn't come out for the rest of the day. He even refused to eat. As time went by, his father became more and more concerned. When the boy refused to come out of the room; even after being threatened, Martin decided something had to be done! The boy would refuse to eat for days at a time. When he was finally, physically forced out of his room; he refused to speak to anyone.

Martin finally made an appointment with a counselor hoping to find help. The counselor was very nice. After a few visits the boy began to open up to her a little. He never revealed the horrors in his life and his past. He focused on the possible future and told her he wanted a happy home. No, it wasn't his sisters' fault; they were always nice to him. He blamed himself for his situation. It was his fault because he was retarded and too stupid to learn; no matter how hard Debra tried to teach him. So he learned to keep his mouth shut. He was never right, anyway. According to Debra, he never had anything important to say. Yes, he had friends. Their names were Peter and Kenny. Their families were different from his. They weren't retarded like him. Oh, the reason he was always in so much trouble was because he was greedy. Debra said he always took the biggest piece of candy or fruit. He had to find a way to keep her from continually accusing him of being greedy and eating all the food. His solution? He simply wouldn't eat! He wasn't necessarily lonely. He just wasn't worthy of love. He hadn't earned it, yet. Maybe, someday, he'd be worthy, but now he wasn't. Oh, he had his invisible friends, but they were more teachers than actual friends. They guided him. They didn't love him either. But they were teaching him how to obey. That was the most important lesson he needed to learn, obedience.

The counselor noticed that every time Debra went to touch the boy, he'd flinch, as if he was about to be hit. When asked why he reacted that way the boy simply replied, "Touching always results in pain and bruises. I prefer not to be touched. Plus, I'm not worthy to be touched. I'm a retard. I'm not even worthy of the air I breathe!" Of course this was true! Debra had repeatedly told him this. She took extreme measures to teach this to him. The counselor asked the boy one more question. "Why do you keep referring to yourself as "the boy" and not by your given name, or nickname?" The counselor told the boy it was common for people, when they meet, to introduce themselves by their names.

"For example, when we met, I said, 'Hello. My name is Donna. What's yours?' You replied, 'I'm the boy.' Why did you respond that way?"

The boy replied, "*I'm not good enough to be called by my name, because it's my father's and my grandfather's name. I'm the boy or that nuisance of a boy or the retard.* I'm a freakin' mental case. I'm not worthy of that name. I'm not even worthy to be called by my original nickname. It belongs to Debra's dog. Even he's better than I am! I'm called, the boy. Don't let Debra hear you call me anything else or she'll discipline you, too!" Finally, after a few more tests, the counselor met with his father and stepmother. The boy was placed in a separate room with toys and games. He wouldn't touch anything, but immediately went to the books where he picked up '*The Bobsie Twins at the Seashore*' and began to read to himself. The staff continued to observe him. Donna, the counselor, spoke with the boy's father and stepmother. She explained to them there was really nothing wrong with the boy's mind. In fact, the tests showed he was above average for his age. He suffered from an inferiority disorder. Because he believed he was mentally disturbed and retarded, he acted that way! Debra was beginning to feel personally attacked. She interrupted the counselor and contentiously said, "I don't know where he would get these ideas from. We don't treat him any different than his sisters."

"Well," observed the therapist, "he seems to feel you don't like him. He doesn't feel he can please you in any way. "

"Oh, that's just utter nonsense!" objected Debra, defiantly. "Can't you see it's just his way of trying to blame anyone else but himself. He just refuses to accept responsibility for his mistakes and will do anything he can to draw attention to himself."

"I don't see it that way at all." remarked the therapist, "In fact, the boy, in spite of his handicap is quite normal in most respects. His reading skills are far above normal!"

"That's impossible!" Debra responded, incredulously. "The boy can't even talk! How can he ever read? How could that even be possible with his disability?"

"Well your time's up." Donna reminded them. "I'd like to schedule a couple of appointments to speak with you, Mrs. Louis, if you don't mind."

That was all Debra could stand to hear. She lost her temper. "Yes! I do mind!" yelled Debra. "It's the boy who has the problems, not me! What kind of therapist are you? How could you think I have a problem?"

"I didn't say you had a problem, Mrs. Louis." Explained the counselor, trying to calm Debra down. "I just asked if we could talk."

"Well, I'll be!" cried Debra, ranting against the counselor. "Martin, take the boy out of here!" She screamed. "I can't understand how they could think the boy was okay and that I, a respectable and mature woman, would have a problem? Are you crazy?" He never saw the counselor again. Things went back to normal for the boy. He learned to adapt to life with Debra.

17
THE ENCOUNTER

One-day something unusual happened. The boy was given a nickel and allowed to go to the corner store to spend it. On the way to the store, a lady; who called him by his nickname, stopped him. This was the name his father and sisters called him. The boy was puzzled. Who was this woman? How did she know his name and what was wrong with her skin? This strange woman asked a question that confused the boy even more. She mentioned his name again and wanted to know if he knew her. She asked him is he knew Jesus yet. He felt himself begin to tremble violently. He could hear his guides screaming not to listen to that awful name. The boy stared straight ahead as if he were in a daze. The lady asked him again if he knew Jesus, yet. He answered back, "Nobody by that name lives in this neighborhood." He didn't know anyone named Jesus. The boy asked the lady who she was and what was wrong with her skin. She asked him, "What do you mean by 'what's wrong with my skin?'"

The boy replied, "Your skin's not like mine. It's black!" The lady laughed, "Oh honey, there's nothing wrong with my skin, that's how God made me."

"Why?" asked the boy?

"Because, God in His wisdom chose to do so, just as He chose to make you the way you are."

"Oh No! God didn't like you either?" questioned the boy.

"What do you mean child?" said the lady.

"Well, God made me a stupid retard, because I was born no good," said the boy.

"Who told you that?" replied the lady.

"My stepmother told me," the boy confessed.

"Oh honey, that's not true! God loves you. What happened to you is not God's fault. It was God who spared your life and He can heal you."

"I don't think God likes me too much lady. Whoever you are."

"Whoever I am? Didn't your daddy ever tell you about me? I'm your mother. I'm Beatrice. Ask you daddy about me." Suddenly, a big man with the same skin problem came up behind the lady. "Oh James!" she cried, "He doesn't know the Lord. He doesn't even know about us!"

"Well, Beatrice, he was only two when we took care of him. And it was only for several months. Now Beatrice, calm down. See how good the Lord is. Look how he directed your steps today in this large city. Your paths crossed! It is a miracle we found him at all! Our God surely withholds nothing! He knows how much you love the boy. He knows how much you pray for him." The lady bent down and hugged him. The big man put his hand on the boy's head and asked the person with the strange name of Jesus to be with this boy. The boy liked the couple, but something inside him feared them. Especially when they would say the name of Jesus whoever that was. As they were about to leave, the woman told the boy to ask his dad about James and Beatrice Wilson. The boy ran home all excited. He couldn't wait to ask his dad about this couple. When he saw his father he ran up to him yelling. "I saw my mother! She has a skin problem! His father told him to calm down. He was hard enough to understand normally, never mind when he got excited. Now what was this nonsense about seeing his mother? The boy told his father all about the couple. He said the woman claimed she was his mother! He also explained that the couple had a skin disease that turned them black! The boy told his father, "The woman's name is Beatrice and the man's name is James. They want to know if I know someone named Jesus!" His father looked down at him and smiled. "I see you met Beatrice. She's not your mother. She just thinks she is. I let her watch you for a while when your mother died. There's nothing wrong with her skin. That's just the way God made her. Her skin is dark because she was born black; just like her husband."

"Daddy, why did God make them so different?"

"I don't know, you should've asked them. They're the religious fanatics, not me."

"Well, daddy, who is this Jesus she was talking about?"

"Son, He's somebody who lived a long time ago. Yes, He was a good man and taught good things. Don't go getting all hung up again about Him and religion. If you're going to be someone or accomplish anything, you and you alone will have to make it happen. With your handicaps, don't worry about doing anything good. Just develop a strong back so you can be a good laborer and make a living. Now, go play. And don't be talking to that crazy couple anymore. They'll just fill your head full of fantasies about God, Heaven and pies in the sky."

"Daddy, don't you believe in God?"

"Of course I do. I believe God made us. He gave us everything we need to survive. Then He left us alone. When we die, if our good deeds outweigh the bad, then we're okay; if not, tough luck! Now get out of here. All this religious talk is foolishness. I'm no preacher. I don't even care about the subject. I got work to do." Then his dad did something unusual. He rubbed the top of the boy's head and said, "Son, you'll never be smart enough to understand the Bible and God. If you try, you'll only be confused and hurt. I know one thing for sure about church and God's so called people. They will be quick to judge and condemn but slow to extend a helping hand. I guarantee every one of them, including their so called God, will let you down!"

"What about the lady and her husband, daddy? They seemed so nice?"

"Well son, they truly are a strange couple. They actually try to live what they claim to believe. You still need to stay away from them. Do you hear me boy?"

"Yes sir!" replied the boy. "I hear you."

"Good, now go outside while you still have time to play," said his dad. The boy ran outside to play with his sisters. While he was playing his guides began to speak to him. They warned him, 'The master doesn't like the couple you were talking to earlier today.' The guides said they were religious fanatics and would cause nothing but trouble with all that nonsense about Jesus. The boy asked his guides, "Who is this Jesus and does He really have the power to heal me?" The guides told the boy Jesus was just a man who lived a long time ago. The boy didn't need to know about Him. In fact, the guide called Ola claimed, "If you want to be healed, then you must obey the master in all things." Then perhaps the boy could earn the right to be healed by proving his worth to the master. "But." said the boy, "The lady was nice. She told me Jesus wasn't dead, but alive! He has the power to heal me and make me normal!"

"Boy, who are you going to believe a crazy woman who thinks she is your dead mother and some dead Jew named Jesus is alive; or your guides? The ones sent by the master to train you are the ones you should believe. Child, as far as power is concerned, would you like a small demonstration of what we can do through you?"

"Yes!" replied the boy, excitedly.

"Then pick up that rock. Hold it in your hands. Now call your sisters to watch." When his sisters arrived, the guides told him to grab the rock with both hands and twist. The boy did what he was told and the rock snapped completely in half. His sisters ran off crying. They were going to tell daddy he was being bad.

"See how easy you broke that stone? Look how your powers frightened your sisters? You don't need some dead Jesus for power! All you need to do is to listen to us and do what you are told. Obey the master and you'll receive all the power you need. Is that clear?" When his guides were done talking the boy's father called him in. He wanted to know what he did to frighten his sisters so much. "I only showed them how strong I was by breaking a rock into two." the boy said, proudly. "That's all I did daddy."

The father laughed and said, "You didn't break that rock in two. Not by your own strength! The rock, more likely, had a crack in it. The crack caused it to break when you put a little pressure on it." The boy simply agreed with his father. He knew better than to argue with him. He couldn't win. He'd only end up with a beating for his effort. The boy went to his room to get ready. About a half hour went by.

Suddenly! He heard a large commotion in the parlor. He ran from his room to see what all the noise was about. The boy was shocked at the sight. His stepmother and sisters were encircled around his father. His father was lying on the floor in convulsions! Finally, after what seemed like forever, his father stopped shaking and slowly regained consciousness. Debra called the doctor after Martin finally was able to sit in his chair. The doctor quickly arrived with his little black bag. He gave Martin a complete physical examination. The doctor explained to Martin. "Mr. Louis, I have bad news for you. It seems you suffer from a medical condition known as Petit Mal Epilepsy. The good news is we can control it with medication. You'll be able to live a nearly normal life because of the advancements modern medicine has made in this field. You'll have to tell your employer about this matter. It will be completely up to them to decide if they'll keep you employed."

"Okay." replied Martin. "I'll let my boss know in the morning. I'll have this prescription filled as soon as possible."

"Good." said the doctor. "I'll give you some medicine to hold you over until your prescription is filled." Everything went back to normal. His employer told Martin he was too valuable to lose. He had a job as long as he wanted as long as the seizures could be controlled with medicine. Life even seemed to improve for the boy. The lack of response to his stepmother's beatings made her lose interest in punishing him. He spent much of his time in his room and out of her way. The boy was only beaten once or twice a week instead of being beaten everyday. He could live with that. Some of his bruises were actually healing and disappearing. His life seemed almost normal.

~ An Easter to Remember ~

Easter (Astarte) was coming again. The boy just received his First Communion and everything seemed to be going along nicely. Maybe this Easter would be fun and he could enjoy it for once. This would prove to definitely be an Easter to remember. On Easter morning, every-thing went as usual. The girls woke up to their Easter baskets and new clothes. The boy received the salt-water taffy he got every year. Surprisingly, he received no threats or beatings this day. Yet, in spite of this good fortune it would be a day to remember forever. Right after the meal his father and Debra began to have an argument. All of a sudden she fell down. She began to shake and convulse as if she was having a seizure like his dad. Martin told his oldest daughter to get a pan of cold water. When she returned with the water, Debra immediately sat right up and came out of her seizure. Martin took the water from his daughter and looked straight at Debra. He told her he wouldn't tolerate being mocked or made fun of because of his epilepsy. What kind of wife would make fun of her husband's serious medical problem? The color drained from Debra's face. She desperately tried to explain what happened. She told Martin she wasn't making fun of his condition.   But because she was so emotionally upset over their disagreement, she fainted. Martin threw the pan of cold water in Debra's face and yelled, "This should calm your emotions down! Debra, it's over! I won't stand for this kind of abuse from my wife. I've been a good husband to you. I've provided all your needs and this is how you repay me!" Martin staggered out of the house. A rebellious wife was not going to embarrass him. "This is the end!"

∼ The Decision ∼

Three days later, the boy and his sisters found themselves standing in front of a man with a black robe and a mallet asking them which parent they wanted to live with; Martin or Debra. The question was easy to answer. They wanted to live with their father. The situation caused another challenge. Now their stepmother wasn't watching the children while Martin worked. Arrangements must be made. In one week's time his sisters were back with his aunt and uncle. A decision still had to be made for the boy.

THE UNHOLY ANOINTING   H.A.LEWIS

18
DADDY DON'T SEND ME AWAY

The boy found himself sitting in an office with a woman dressed in a strange outfit. Everybody called her "Mother Superior." There were other women called nuns. They were telling his father they'd take good care of the boy. Yes, they were aware of his handicaps. Yes, he'd get along just fine with the other children. Of course, Martin would be allowed to visit and even take the boy out on weekends. The boy sat quietly, staring at these strange women. They were all dressed the same way. They looked like a small group of pigeons in their black and white outfits. The large wooden crucifixes hanging around their necks fascinated the boy. He took great pain to notice the man; beaten and hanging on the cross.

Suddenly, the boy could clearly hear the voice of his guides telling him the man hanging on the cross was the mysterious, legendary Jesus of Nazareth. "See?" said the guide, "Did we not tell you He was dead? Look on every cross these fools have draped around their necks. You find Him hanging there crucified for the entire world to see. How can this Jesus be more powerful than the master? You don't see the master hanging on a cross, beaten, and naked; an embarrassment to everyone who sees it! Young man," said the guide. "Don't let these foolish women in their ridiculous outfits deceive you into believing their silly stories and religious fairy tales. Jesus was a good man who lived a long time ago. Granted, he was a great teacher, but so were Buddha, Confucius, and Mohammed. They all taught religious principles and even wrote some of those so called 'Holy Books.' All roads lead to God. Don't let anyone convince you of some narrow-minded concept claiming Jesus is the only way to God. Boy, as you can see, these ignorant nuns wear a dead idol around their necks. Jesus is heading nowhere. How could He be the only way to God? Now child, do you understand what we're telling you?"

"Yes I do." replied the boy. "I thank you for being patient with me and showing me the truth. I'll never doubt your words. I will obey the master faithfully in all things."

"Very good child," said Ola the guide. "He'd expect no less from his only son." Martin met with the nuns at the orphanage for a while. Then he took the boy out for pizza. He explained to the boy that his aunt and uncle thought it was unfair to his grandparents for the boy to live with them. It was okay for him. He was grown and no one had to watch him. Since the boy was handicapped and so young, they felt he'd be too much trouble for his grandparents. It'd be for the best. He'd be committed for a while in the orphanage. His father could visit him on weekends. When the boy was of age he'd be released.

"Daddy, don't you love me? Are you mad at me because of Debra? Is it my fault you left? I'm sorry. I don't mean to be a bad boy. I love you. I'll try to be good. ***Please, don't send me away!*** I don't like those ladies with the dead Jesus hanging around their necks. They look so mean."   The other children look so unhappy and they don't like me! One of the older boys told me there's hardly enough food and clothes for everybody. The nuns are always punishing the children, especially the new ones. He said that since I talk so funny and have a hard time playing, that all the other kids would pick on me. Also, Daddy, he said if I don't do well in school, I'll have to see the priest and he'll beat me for being stupid!"

Martin answered, "Son, stop this foolish talking! That boy was only teasing you. It won't be for long and it definitely won't be that bad. Now, when we arrive at the house tonight, you be quiet while I talk to your grandparents. I'll need to discuss what's going on."

～ The discussion now began ～

Martin and his son arrived at his parent's home. Martin was facing a dilemma and didn't know what to do. He came to his parent's home to seek their guidance. When they arrived, they settled in the living room. A few moments later his mom asked them to come to the table. Dinner was ready. Martin explained the plan he had for his son to his parents over dinner. The boy was completely caught off guard. For the first time ever in his young life, he saw his grandfather become angry. Martin's father shouted, "I am so sick of you all telling me how much trouble that child is because of his handicap. That boy tries with all his heart to overcome his weakness. This is my home and he's always invited here. You tell that brother of yours and his loud mouth wife to stay out of my business and that goes double for your sister and her husband. They don't want the boy to be a burden to me? Trust me, Martin, when they need something, they don't worry about burdening me. They don't hesitate to ask for it! Your brother still owes me thousands of dollars. He borrows and never pays it back. Your sister lives well because we were there when they needed help. How soon they forget! I'll tell you this only once, Martin! If you ever put my grandson in an orphanage, you'll never be welcome in my house again! I'll always have a grandson, but if you do this thing, I won't always have a son. Is my meaning clear? Martin nodded.

His father continued assuring him saying," Martin, you work and you help. This child doesn't take up much space. He doesn't eat a lot and I enjoy my daily walk with him."

Martin objected. "But Dad, you and mom are getting on in age and a young child under foot, adding to the noise and distractions, isn't good for you."

Martin's mother spoke up. "Martin, stop this nonsense now! Your father has spoken. This is our home. Not yours or your brothers or sisters. I am in total agreement with your father. As far as I am concerned, his word is law. It's final in this house. Now, if you think that orphanage is so great; then you live there! You will not put our grandson there! As far as we're concerned, this child has been through enough trouble in his young life. Enough is enough! You will not expose him to that institution! Our home will be his security. You know your father and I weren't in agreement with you and your brother married outside of our faith. It was your choice and we didn't interfere with your decision to raise your children in that church. But, we draw the line here. The boy is loved and wanted. You don't need to put him there."

"OK!" said Martin, "I just didn't want to be a burden to you."

"Martin, it's our decision. We decide if you're a burden on us or not. Do you understand? It's not anyone else's business. Now, you remember that boy's family. He's our blood. He'll never be a burden." The horrible secret which had lasted five long years was now unveiled. It was not a secret any longer. Debra's horrible mistreatment of the boy was finally brought to light. "Martin, I now see how you and everyone treat this boy as if he'll never amount to anything. Stop it! Stop it now! Quit listening to his voice! Instead, look into his eyes and see the strong spirit the good Lord has given him. *This child will amaze us all someday. I am proclaiming it!*"

"Mom, you are free to believe what you want. I choose to face reality. My son is handicapped and you can pray all you want to your God. It'll make no difference. Your so-called God of mercy took my wife, Mary and my son, Michael, and left this one handicapped."

"Martin," said his Mom, "you know I love you. You're welcome here, as Dad and I have said. There's one rule that I will not compromise. No one will speak evil of my God in my house! It's because of His mercy and grace that your boy is alive. Quit blaming Him for the death of your wife. God didn't make her abuse herself with alcohol. She did! We were helpless to stop her. You can't blame God for our mistakes or shortcomings. I loved Mary very much, but you know she didn't take care of herself."

"OK Mom." replied Martin. "No more talk about Mary. It still hurts. It's only been seven years. I still miss her. I know not to argue religion with you. In fact, you're as bad as Beatrice and James are, with their constant efforts to convert me."

"Mom, I won't speak against your God in your home," said Martin. "In fact, you raised me to believe in God. As far as I am concerned, God is God and He is free to do what he wants. But, I don't believe He personally cares about us. He gave us life and left us alone to live it as best as we can. I won't beg Him for handouts. When I stand before Him I'll stand in my own strength. I won't blame Him for my failures or my successes. As far as I'm concerned, I walk alone! I'm responsible for my success or failures. Not God, not the devil, not you. Am I clear?"

"Martin, I'll never understand why you hardened your heart and turned from faith in God to unbelief. I always felt you were called to preach. But now I wonder if you ever had a relationship with God. It's different than serving a religion, you know."

"Mom, let's not go there. Let this conversation end now! I don't want to upset you. I love you. But I don't see God as you see Him."

"Martin." His mother interrupted, "May I take the boy to church once in a while?"

"Yes, Mom, you may; if he chooses to go. Please remember, I gave my word to Mary and I'll keep it. He will be raised in her church as I have promised. Is that clear and understood?"

"Yes, Martin. Good night for now."

19
STRATEGY

The boy slept silently for the first time in a long time. His guides stood at the foot of the bed discussing the boy. While he slept, the guides known as Chango and Ola discussed his adventure.

Ola said to Chango, "The master is upset that his plans for the boy were altered. It would have been perfect if the boy had been placed in the orphanage. He would have been treated horribly and the master could have molded his young mind so strongly against the Christian God by using that so called Christian (religious) institution. It would have completely turned him off to Christianity."

"Everything is not lost!" said Chango. "The boy's still going to be allowed to attend the same dead church his mother was raised in. That church where Christ still hangs on the cross holds no evidence of his power and authority. It isn't a church where the blood is honored, or even mentioned! Nor the Holy Spirit taught. It's a legalistic church with many rules and no joy. All they had to do was keep him there and his damnation would be assured; all by works and no grace."

"I must admit Chango," said Ola to his partner," this was an absolute masterpiece. The way you used the crucifix, the boy saw hanging around the nuns' neck, to convince him Jesus was only a man; and not God manifested in the flesh. You truly had the boy believing Jesus was dead, just as Mohammad and Buddha are. All religions have the same end. Just the names are different."

"Yes Ola." said Chango. "Greater minds than this boy have died believing this lie. It makes the master laugh when these so-called theologians and educators, these foolish, pious, religious hypocrites hold firmly to this religious lie. It never ceases to amaze me to see the surprise on their self-righteous faces when they find out the truth; too late! Mankind is truly a strange creature. *He'll worship anything but the one true God!* It is so strange. No matter what foolishness the master puts them through, as long as they feel they alone know a mysterious secret, *they'll swallow any lie. Yes, no matter how simple the truth, in their ignorance and pride they'll struggle to receive it.* It really doesn't matter Ola. It all works in our favor. As the master said, we'll conquer these foolish humans and once more walk the celestial streets of our original home; where the master rules from his righteous throne!"

"Chango, do you truly believe this?" asked Ola.

"Yes Ola." replied Chango. "You better believe it, too! What other hope do we have? If the master is wrong, **THEN ALL IS LOST**, and we are as foolish and blind as these mere religious mortals! If the master is wrong, then we've gambled everything and lost it all. We have actually given up heaven to embrace damnation! No more of this talk. If the master even senses we may doubt the outcome of his battle with the Nazarene; we'll pay a terrible price for our lack of trust in the master's ultimate plan. For now, Ola, we will continue to deceive the boy in every way possible until he fulfills the master's goal for his life. When he's done all of the master's desire and fulfilled his usefulness to our kingdom; then you Ola, Great Spirit of death, may do with him whatsoever you please. You may destroy him any way you wish!"

Ola announced, "That will be a great day. But until then, Chango, I will take great pleasure in afflicting him with as much torment as I can. Was it not glorious to observe all the pain his stepmother put him through for those five years he lived with her? All would be perfect if it were not for his grandparents and those two obstinate prayer warriors praying, constantly, for the boy."

"Yes Ola." said Chango, "James and Beatrice are definitely a clog in the master's plan for the life of this flesh bag. Why the master tolerates their interference with their persistent praying, I will never understand. People like these two confuse me at times. They make me feel as if those who are called deceivers are actually being deceived themselves. I have personally tried to come against their foolish prayers; to silence them once and for all. Every time I'm near them I can feel the power of the enemy surrounding them. I have seen the army of the heavenly host circling around them. I stand amazed at our former brothers. They cannot see the true self-centered plans of the Creator. He made man a little lower than us for a season, but some day according to that terrible Book, they'll be greater than us! They'll rule and reign, supposedly, with the Messiah forever! We, who were created, first, will have to serve them and be judged by them! Where is the fairness in that? Why our brothers would settle for being second best, I'll never understand. Why they refuse to join our worthy cause is beyond my comprehension. We owe so much to the master. It was he who dared to take a stand against the oppression of the Creator. He refused to live an existence of eternal slavery to a Creator who didn't appreciate loyalty and refused to exalt him to his rightful position. I hear so many of these so-called Christians speaking about our master's greed, questioning why he couldn't settle for being second best, and why he dared to take a chance to raise himself from slave to kingship. How dare they question our master's quest for advancement? These little hypocrites bite and devour themselves in order to rise to the top in their self imposed little earthly kingdoms of clay. If it weren't for that blasphemous Michael, we'd be ruling, openly, from the heavenly kingdom! Instead, we're bound in shadows and secrecy in the darkness surrounding this hunk of mud called the earth. Curse that lapdog Michael for not minding his own business! The master would have given him a position of importance in the new kingdom; he'll have after his glorious victory.

"Well, I'll tell you one thing Ola." Reminded Chango. "The master will not be caught off guard a second time by a mere creation, whether it is an archangel or some-thing else."

"What do you mean, a second time, Chango?" asked Ola.

"Didn't the Nazarene, in the temptation in the desert, catch the master off guard? Wasn't our advancement to victory pushed back by the victory of Jesus the Christ?"

"Watch your mouth Ola!" demanded Chango. "You sound almost like a follower of this so-called Messiah. You know it was only a temporary setback. The master will recover and will accomplish his glorious plan. Ola, keep in mind, it's been nearly 2000 years since the birth of the Church, and except for the first couple of centuries, they've accomplished very little. His followers have this so-called power of the Spirit given to them to conquer us. Still they've had little success against our weapons. Rest assured Ola, Great Spirit of the dead, we won't have to conquer them. They'll defeat themselves with all their petty jealousy towards one another. Wasn't it their own Founder of the so-called Church who stated, 'How can a kingdom, divided against itself, stand?' All we have to do is keep them filled with pride and jealousy and they will do our job for us. Well, Ola, the day is almost here and the boy is beginning to wake. Let us step back into the shadow to continue to carry out the master's orders for his life."

The boy woke fully rested for the first time in years. As he began to dress, he could sense that he had visitors during the night. The atmosphere of the room was filled with the electricity, which was always left behind after his guides visited. He was puzzled why they hadn't awakened him. Normally, they didn't allow him to sleep when they were around. They constantly stressed the importance of his training. They said there would come a time when he could rest all he wanted. But until then, his training was more important. So why didn't they wake him? A strange thought came to the boy. It seemed when he was in his grandfather's house, his guides seemed to be limited in their ability to manifest and communicate. It was as if a stronger spirit and guide were present. They couldn't stand against it. He'd seen the guides' reaction when his grandparents read from the black Book. When the two would pray his guides would always make excuses to leave. The boy noticed something else. He noticed the master couldn't make an appearance in his grandfather's home. The boy would ask the guides why when he met with them.

~~ It was a great Day! ~~

It was a great day knowing that the boy and his father were going for a long walk. His father gave him a small plastic airplane he found while they were walking near his father's work. Martin took the boy inside and showed him the building He introduced the boy to the people he worked with. On the way home, Dad gave him some news. He'd be together with his sisters, soon. He'd found a place for them all to live together as a family once again; and nothing will ever separate them! His heart regretted leaving the place he loved the best. But, the boy was happy because his father was happy. He wanted to be with his sisters and be a family again.

Nevertheless, he didn't want to leave his grandfather's home. It was truly a place of peace for him. The only real home he had ever known in his young life. What will this new place be like? Perhaps he could live with his grandparents and visit with his family on weekends? Later the next day, as he went for his daily walk with his grandfather, he asked if it would be possible for him to remain with his grandparents. His grandfather replied he'd love to have the boy stay with him. But, told him his father wanted them all to be together as a family at last. Martin was truly looking forward to it. The boy understood. He didn't want to disappoint his father. It would be great to be a family once again. He could always visit his grandparents on the weekends.

20
THE PROJECTS - A WHOLE NEW WORLD

The big day came. The boy found himself in an apartment in the projects. The place was clean and nice. There were plenty of other children his age to make friends with. There were elderly neighbors on either side of his apartment. They appeared to be nice. The place was actually better than he imagined it would be. His sisters already made friends with the older children in the projects. His father, due to his size, won favor with the adults. Maybe it won't be too hard to make friends. The boy soon found things were different in the projects. Much different from his grandparents. At his grandparents, you just made friends with the other kids in the neighborhood. Sometimes you got into fights, but you got over it and went on with life. Not here! Not in the projects. You don't just make friends. If you get into a fight, it's not just with one person. It may involve one person, but includes all of his friends and relatives. If you aren't a member of a gang, life can be extremely difficult. You find yourself fighting every day just to survive.

The boy eventually won enough fights to be left alone by most of the gang members. It seemed that almost everyone in the projects except, for his family; were somehow related to each other. They only respect power and brute force! It is rule through intimidation. The boy's family was quickly accepted

105

because of an incident that occurred shortly after they moved in. The boy's older sister came home with a friend. She was crying. Her father asked what happened. She told him nothing and ran into the apartment. When her father asked her friend, she told him the Shakley brothers had called her a whore and threatened to slap her if she didn't do what they told her. The girl told Martin everyone feared the Shakley brothers because of their size. They both stood well over six feet tall and over 300 pounds. They'd never been beaten in a fight. People just stood clear and avoided any conflict with them. Martin stood up and told the young girl, "I guess it all ends today. Nobody insults my daughter!" Martin walks to the front of the projects where the Shakley's live. The news spreads like wildfire. The new man is going to confront the Shakley's. People try to stop Martin; to tell him how dangerous these men are. The police won't attempt to arrest them. Since no harm was really done to his daughter, they feel he should just leave it alone. People will understand.

Martin arrives at the brother's home to a large crowd quickly gathering. Martin approaches the two men. An elderly woman steps between Martin and the brothers. She tells Martin to be wise and turn around. "Forget what happened and go home. These two men are my sons and they're mean. They won't think twice about really hurting you. No one has been able to deal with them since they were teenagers. They take advantage of their great size and have never been beaten by anyone!"

Martin just smiles and asks the lady to move out of his way. The mother of the two men moves aside. The brothers rise to their full height. Both men are very physically impressive. They are completely confident in their size. They know everyone in the crowd fears them. When they are done with this pest no one will tell the cops anything. Martin asks them to apologize to his daughter. They simply laugh and tell him they don't apologize to whores. They warn Martin, that if he's smart, to turnaround and walk home before he has to be carried home! The boy is afraid for his father. He knows Martin won't back down. What chance does he have against these two monsters? In the boy's mind it's like Batman trying to take on Godzilla and King Kong by himself. He can sense that everyone in the crowd thinks his father is doomed. These two giants are in their early twenties and Martin is forty-two! What chance does he have? The boy prays that his uncle will come in time. Then at least his father will have help. His uncle is over 300 pounds and solid as a rock. The chances will be so much better. But, his uncle isn't here, though. He won't arrive in time. He's on his way. But he won't arrive in time. The boy's sister called and told him what was happening. But he will arrive too late. It will be over before he can reach his brother's side to help.

Martin ignores the Shakley's threat. Once again, he asks for an apology to be made to his daughter. The Shakley's mother says she'll apologize. Martin tells her, "Thank you, but you aren't the one who made the statement." She isn't the one who needs to make the apology. Then he gives them one more chance to apologize. Martin asks, "Which one made the insult?" His daughter points at the bigger older brother. She says he called her a whore and the other brother threatened to slap her. "Ok." Martin says to the older brother. 'Then I'll deal with you, first!"

The big man laughs and roars like an angry beast, "I'll break you in half and toss your broken body to my brother to play with." he screams as he rushes toward Martin. But he never reaches him.

Martin threw two punches that day and both men fell. They were knocked out cold. Martin had shattered both their jaws! The police arrived twenty minutes later. Both men were still out cold. They had to be transported by ambulance to the hospital. Their mother was amazed. From that day forward no one bothered him. Martin left the projects twenty years later, untouched. He became a living legend among the people. Until the day Martin died, people continued to talk about the lightening fists of Martin Louis. Everything went back to normal after the Shakley incident. His sisters were well

107

accepted. But the boy, because of his speech problem, was having difficulty getting by. The boy had only two things that helped him. He was the son of Martin Louis and he could also hold his own in a fight.

<h2 align="center">~~ Like father, like son ~~</h2>

Shortly, after the incident with the Shakley brothers, the boy was caught on the wrong side of the projects with two of his friends the gang considered to be nerds. The boy was forced to fight two brothers who were leaders in the gang. The two friends ran. The boy was left to face the two brothers, alone. The fight didn't last long. The boy was filled with pent-up anger and took it out on the two brothers. The day was almost over. Not only had he beaten the brothers, but a large part of the gang!

<h2 align="center">~~ His Initiation ~~</h2>

Later that night, the gang leader and warlord approached the boy. He asked if he wanted to be a member. He replied, "Yes." After a full initiation, he became a member of "Hell's Kitchen's Finest." The boy experienced his first gang war soon after he joined. Hell's Kitchen was in a battle with a gang from East High. One of the girls had been slapped and insulted by a member of the East High gang. The reputation of the projects rode on the incident. Eighty-two members of the gang went to East High. They left a mess when they were done. It was carnage! Bodies' lay everywhere. Cars were vandalized. Windows in cars and houses were broken. Yards were trashed. The gang had its revenge. The boy proved to be a great addition to the gang, with a tire iron for a weapon. He added to the number of victims who were beaten. The gang rejoiced after each battle and celebrated with a big beer party. The account of the battle grew larger each time they told it. They told it over and over again. It was presented in viciousness. The adults victoriously joined in the celebration.

Martin was again famous in the community. Martin made war clubs for each of the members. He made them all by hand in his cellar. He showed them how to use trashcan covers as shields .He said only a coward would run from the heat of battle. The gang told Martin how proud they were to have his son battle with them. They bragged about what he did and how he seemed to be transformed into a different person, altogether. For the first time; Martin told the boy he was proud of him. It was funny. The boy always felt if Martin was his age; he'd be the gang's leader. The members were always around him and listened to what he had to say. In fact, he spent more time with them, showing them how to do things from working on cars, televisions, radios, and making weapons; than he did with his own son. The only way the boy seemed to get Martin's attention was if he was vicious and victorious in battle. The only topic Martin ever talked about was fighting and war in the army. He was always teaching the boy about military intelligence. He said that real men never show emotions. They ignored pain at all costs. It seemed as if he was trying to train the boy for *Special Forces.*

~~ The Ambush ~~

One day the boy was coming home. Nearly seven members of a rival black gang ambushed him. They attacked him near the front steps, where his Dad and their dog were sitting. The boy fought frantically to defend himself against the great odds. His father just sat and watched as always. He watched his son transform into another person. The boy was normally shy and quiet, but in battle he became an animal. That day, while his father watched the battle, his dog saw his buddy in trouble and came to his aid grabbing one of the rival gang members by the throat. The boy was finally able to defeat his opponents, although out numbered. The boy dusted himself off and picked up his dog and embraced him. He went to his father and asked why he didn't help him. He asked him, "Why didn't you stand up and help me?" All Martin had to do was stand up and those coming after the boy would have turned away. He knew they feared him.

Martin looked at the boy and simply said, "You're a Louis. Remember that! No matter what, a Louis never needs help from anyone. You won. Didn't you? If I'd helped you, then you'll never know what you could have done. Besides, you weren't alone. The dog was with you." Martin would never show emotion to the boy. Martin was different with his daughters. He was open, loving and gentle. Martin's emotions were different with his son. He treated him differently. His temper would rise and he would become very angry. He took out his anger on the boy until he was exhausted. One time, he beat the boy so badly he couldn't walk for two weeks. That day, he beat the boy until he fell; and then kept kicking him until he heard something snap in the boys back.

Another incident came about. The boy was once again being blamed. Martin reacted in the same way he always did; with his fists. Martin grabbed him and beat him. He didn't look into the story right away. When he finally did, he found out the boy was innocent of the charges he was beaten for. His reaction to the boy was. "You're innocent of this, but I know there's something I owe you a beating for." That was the closest to an apology the boy would ever receive. It seemed his father took the place of his stepmother. Transference took place in order to have the master's job done in his life. Although it didn't happen every day, violence was no stranger to the boy's life. It was hard, but it was better than his stepmother's house where he was constantly abused. In fact, the boy reached a point in his life when he no longer feared the physical beatings. Pain could be managed and turned into power.

The boy learned from his guides. If he endures the pain and gives in to his anger; incredible power will come forth. He will actually become someone else in the mist of battle!

It was as if someone entered into him and took over him at times. He felt like the cartoon character, the incredible Hulk. Anger turned this mild mannered scientist into a rampaging monster of awesome power; which no one could stop. The guides told him it was not a monster inside. The boy was getting in touch with his true self.

The warrior within could be called upon at any time to help the boy. This happened many times when he reached a certain point of anger. He'd literally see red and black out. The battle would be over and he wouldn't remember anything.

21
LOSS OF A FRIEND

Life had become so strange for him since moving into the projects. He and his sisters were together, but they seldom saw each other. His sisters hung around with older gang members. This was not the family life he dreamed about. Certainly not the life he had with his grandfather. He didn't get along with a lot of the gang members because of his speech problems. He avoided contact with them as much as possible. He was also losing contact with his grandfather. He hadn't seen him in months. His father promised he could spend weekends at his grandparents, but he hadn't kept his promise. Another challenge came to his father. His father had a seizure on the job. This cost him his job. The doctors said his type of epilepsy could not be controlled enough to guarantee he could safely work without further incident. So now, his father was on disability. To make matters worse, on Thanksgiving Day, while in transit to his aunt's house, his father had a terrible accident with all of them in the car. The authorities took his license from him because they declared it was dangerous for him to operate a vehicle because of his epilepsy.

His father's anger was increasing and the beatings came more frequently now. His father blamed the boy for all of the problems in his life; for any reason it seemed. The boy couldn't remember the last time his father reached out to him in gentleness. It truly frustrated the boy to see how loving and tender his father was toward his sisters. Their needs were barely being met. They needed extra finances. The boy's father asked the boy to help out and go to work. He pursued some opportunities and found a job on the farm. All summer the boy worked on farms for six days a week from 7 am to 7 pm. For this he received $9.00 as pay; for the entire week. Every Saturday when he came home he had to give his sisters $3.00 each. On Sunday, he had to do the laundry, the shopping, and clean the house. When he asked his father why, he got slapped in the face just for asking. He was told it was his responsibility as the man to provide for the house and not his sisters. His father was no longer the man he used to know. He was completely different with everybody else, but the boy. His father was known for his extreme kindness and willingness to help. He had many times given away the week's groceries to other families who were facing hard times. He always had time to take care of the hurts of any of the children in the projects, or to fix any broken toy or television brought to him from others. His hands were always gentle when he held his neighbors children, but was hard when dealing with his own son.

The boy and Martin would sit for hours without speaking to each other. When the boy became sick, his father would never touch him. Once the boy was very sick. He lay alone on the couch for four days fighting a severe fever. His older sister tried to feed him some soup. After the second day they begged his father to call the doctor; which he refused to do. He told her the boy would get over it. He said most of it was just a big show for attention. The boy had to learn to be a man and not give in to these things. Only one time, during those four days, did he even come close to the boy. Every time the boy did become ill, no matter how serious it was, he was always made to feel he was a major inconvenience to the family. He soon learned to stay away from the house as much as possible. He stayed in his room when he was home, away from everyone. Just when life seemed it couldn't get worse, his father received bad news. The boy's grandfather was in the hospital and in bad shape. For the first time, in a long time, the boy saw emotion on his father's face. Martin couldn't believe something bad could ever happen to his father. The boy couldn't believe something bad could happen to his grandfather.

~~ The sudden loss of his best friend ~~

Martin spent the next three days at the hospital. One night, Martin came home and told the children their grandfather had died. He told the boy he was a man. He could be a pallbearer at his grandfather's funeral. The memory of the funeral and carrying his grandfather's casket carved a hole in his heart. *His grandfather was the only friend he had.* The cold grave helped kill whatever feelings or emotions were left in the heart of the boy. He didn't care what happened. Now he knew feelings and emotions were only for girls and the weak. Men didn't show emotion and didn't give in to pain. From that day, when he buried his grandfather, his only true friend, he felt he buried himself. The abuse continued and the beatings increased. But he never again let his father see him cry. Something died within the boy on the day he buried his grandfather. It wasn't just coldness in his heart, but there was darkness in his soul that wouldn't leave until many years later. Shortly after the death of his grandfather, the boy's grandmother passed away. He was a pallbearer for her funeral, also. As he set her down, by the side of his grandfather's grave, the boy made a vow to the vast unknown. **He would never love again!** *His father was absolutely correct.* ***Feelings were totally useless and only got in the way.***

~~ The increase of new power ~~

From that time on the activities of the guides, which were his mentors, increased. Now they began to appear to the boy nightly, constantly teaching the old ways. The boy was able to more easily move objects with his mind. He started first by rolling pencils around. He then moved glasses and finally he was able to slam doors shut with his mind. *The boy was afraid of his new power at first.* But, the mentors shortly convinced him there was nothing to be afraid of. **These were just spiritual gifts he was born with**. The master had chosen him to be a vessel of honor for his kingdom. When the time was right he'd be baptized in power with the anointing of the master to carry out his will. There was more to learn in order for this to happen. These things were still future. The boy needed to concentrate on serving the master, now.

Something came over the boy. He manifested another attitude, another spirit. He began to offer sacrifices to the master. At first, it was simply frogs. He'd torture and then kill the creatures. He must have killed hundreds of them. He skinned many alive before offering them to the master. Eventually the boy moved up to larger sacrifices. He became a skillful hunter. The boy was overcome by violence more and more. In gang fights he was often the first in and the last to leave. Even his own members didn't feel safe near him in a fight. He was just as liable to hit one of them as to hit a rival gang member. The boy was no longer backing down from the older members of the gang anymore. He even got into a fight with the leader of the older gang who had bullied him for a long time. The members of his group literally had to tear him off of the bully. The boy was crazy and lashing out at everyone. Then something very strange and eerie happened. The boy was at the gang's headquarters talking with a group of members. One of the members kept interrupting the meeting. He was trying to take over. He was very large youth standing well over six feet tall and weighed over 220 pounds. He felt, because of his size, he should be the new leader. Three times he interrupted the boy. Finally, the boy spoke to him saying, "Sammy, next time you interrupt me, I'll break your leg! Do you understand me?"

Sammy just laughed saying, "You couldn't break your own leg you skinny little punk. If you don't shut up, I'll break your jaw, you freak!"

The next event frightened everybody at the hangout. The boy just stared at Sammy and quietly spoke, **"LEG BE BROKEN!"** And a loud snap was heard throughout the headquarters as Sammy's leg broke in three places! Years later when these two met as men, Sammy still used a cane to walk. The leg never healed right. The boy learned thoughts and spoken words are powerful; and can bring manifestation!

22
PROVEN WORTHY

That night, after everything had settled down and the boy was alone in his room; his guides appeared. They were angry with the boy for losing control of his power. They warned the boy the power was not for his use alone, but to glorify the master. He was never to use it for his own purpose. Just as easily as the power was given to him, it could be taken away if he abused it. The master wants no unnecessary attention brought to the boy. Therefore, he's required to be in complete control of his gifts at all times. The master wants him to have control over his temper. He doesn't need enemies at his back door. The master knows the boy is drinking and using foul language in public. He doesn't show respect for any authority. The master demands he stop all of this foolishness! Doesn't the boy know who he truly is? Does he think this man, Martin, is his real father? Doesn't he know the master is his sire, the one who gave him life? He is the son of Shiva, the God of Destruction! Doesn't he understand his foolishness and raging temper are bringing embarrassment to his father's kingdom? The boy must learn to be responsible and act properly at all times. He is meant to be a leader and not a follower. The boy asked the guides a few simple questions. "If Shiva is my father, and he is so powerful, why does he allow me to suffer so much? Why should I care about him? Where was he when my mother died? Where was he when I was dying? Where was he

119

when I was being abused and hurting? What kind of a father lets his son suffer when he could have helped?"

The guide told the boy, "Watch how you speak about the great Shiva. He can destroy you at will and raise up another in your place! Shiva has his reasons for not interfering in your life. If he keeps helping you all the time, you'll never gain the spiritual strength you need to lead your father's followers. Even the thorns in your flesh are part of Shiva's plan to make your strong as iron; from the weakness of your handicap. The 'iron' the master desires is forged in deep adversity. The way people react to you will cause you to grow stronger than your enemies. This will be proof you have the spirit to be a leader in your father's army. Can't you see Shiva's testing is needed to make you the warrior you're meant to be? The unnecessary emotion called love can never accomplish this. Love usually gets in the way of victory. What good did it do the hero? He sacrificed his life for those he loved. What victory came through the sacrifice? The hero was still dead! What benefit is this great offering to him personally? So what if a group of ungrateful self-centered people is saved and enjoying life? He lays cold and forgotten in a dark grave, with only a lonely stone marker to keep him company." The guide continued, "Oh, young man, do not be so foolish as to be blinded by the silly emotion called love. Live your life for your father and his kingdom. Everything he owns will be yours. If you perish while loyally building his empire, know this; not only will you be remembered in his kingdom for your valiant actions, but you his son, will rule and reign with him! So be mindful; your father knows what he's doing and it's not for you to question him on anything; ever! Your only purpose is to obey him; no matter what the cost to you! Am I clearly understood on this?" asked the guide.

"Yes." replied the boy. "I understand completely. My life is not my own. The only reason to live is to serve my father and to build his kingdom. I will never question anything and obey in all things. The flesh is but a house of clay and is only temporary. My spirit and mind are eternal and those are not to be weak. Please, forgive me oh great master and help me to obtain wisdom and spiritual strength; that my master may be glorified in everything I do. From this moment forward I shall not doubt and I shall hail him to whom all glory is due!"

"Very good!" replied the guides. "Your answer will bring great joy to your father's heart. You have proven your worthiness to be his son."

"One last question? May I ask one last question before you leave?' the boy replied.

"Of course," said the guides.

"If Shiva is my father and he is king, then I am a prince. Is this not so?"

"Why, yes." replied the guide. "This is true."

"So if Shiva is king. Then all things are subjected to him, including the prince. Is this not so?"

"Yes, you are once again correct," said the guide. The boy was thinking all of this through. He said, "So, that means all things are first subjected to the king, and then to the prince, who is the son of the king. So that means, dear guides, you are not over me, but I am over you. Therefore, I do not ask but demand respect from you. From this day forth when you speak to me, I am not your slave, but your monarch. Only Shiva is above me. Since I bear his name and his mark on my arm; I also bear his power and authority! You are subjected to me! You do not order me. I order you! I carry his authority!"

A look of great hate crossed the face of the guide as he reached for his sword. The mentor became angry and said, "You insolent arrogant piece of clay. I will teach you to disrespect me." Just as the sword began to clear its hilt a voice bellowed from behind the boy. 'Ola, spirit of the dead, you would touch your prince, the son of your master? Would you also draw your sword against me, your master, because I rule over you?"

Great fear came over the face of the guide called Ola saying, "Oh, great master, this is not what it appears. I did not draw my sword to strike my prince; who is the son of my great king and master. I drew it to anoint him as a great warrior who is proven by his words he spoke today."

"Oh?" replied Shiva. "Then go and anoint him before my eyes, Ola, spirit of the dead, and then kneel before him as all must do. Remember, Ola, do not dare even for a mere second to forget this young man is my son. What so ever you do to him you do to me. So if any dare to strike him, they dare to strike me! Is this not true?"

"Oh yes, great master. I was just giving honor to the boy."

"He is no longer a boy." spoke the master. "He is a young man, and will be treated as one. You will personally see to it. Is that understood, Ola?"

"Oh yes, master!"

"One more thing. I'm holding you, *Ola, spirit of the dead*; personally responsible for anything that happens to my son from this moment on. Now, leave us before my moment of generosity dissolves and I test the strength of your sword with that of mine! I will have time with my son, alone!" bellowed Shiva once again. In less than a heartbeat, Ola vanished, leaving the young man with the spirit called Shiva; who claimed to be his father. "I see the feature of your mother in you, young man; her hair and her eyes. Is her faithfulness and her loyalty there as well?" questioned Shiva.

"Yes, my Lord." replied the young man while kneeling in the presence of this magnificent creature. "*My life is yours to do with as thou please.* Father, if I have offended our servant, Ola, Great Spirit of the dead; forgive me. I do not wish to be out of line with your authority. You've placed him over me to teach me and lead me and I will submit and learn."

"You were not wrong, my son. You are a prince and they are your subjects. Ola, at times forgets who rules, and needs to be reminded of his position in my kingdom. But, never take it upon yourself to challenge those whom I send to you! They are great warriors who have earned their place of authority through their obedience and loyalty. You must not disrespect them! Am I clear in this?"

"Yes, master." replied the young man.
"I am your father, young man. Why do you refer to me as master?"

"Yes, my Lord, you are my father. But, first and foremost you are my lord and master. I desire to show you reverence and remind myself never to take that for granted in our relationship."

"You have learned well, young man. You will show your ability to lead by willingly placing yourself under authority. You will not, arrogantly, demand a position in my kingdom. Do not worry about Ola. I will speak to him. I am sure he won't hold anything against you. Now, before I leave, is there anything you want from me?"

"Yes, master. Clarity of mind and understanding is what I want so I may serve you better."

"Once again, I am pleased with your response. I shall grant this now. Be busy and go increase my kingdom." Quicker than the young man could blink the master was gone and the young man was once again alone. Disturbing news came three days later to Martin. His young daughter was with child! His world was turned upside down. The seriousness of his epilepsy caused him to lose his job and rely on veteran's aid; which just about supplied the needs of the family. This unexpected news sent him into a rage. It wasn't against his daughter, but against the man who touched her. When Martin caught the young man, it took the entire older gang to tear him off. The man laid in the middle of the street; bleeding heavily from his mouth. Martin repeatedly kicked him in the head and stomach. Finally the members of the gang were able to bring Martin under control. He almost killed him! When the police arrived, the group of young men told the officers a stranger came through the projects looking for a fight. Because Martin was alone and older, he must have thought he'd be an easy victim. He picked the wrong person! The police didn't believe the story but didn't have any choice but to accept it. These officers knew Martin. They knew no one in their right mind would choose him as a victim. After being examined at the local hospital, it was determined the man suffered a broken nose, jaw, and all of the ribs on one side of his body were fractured. He was lucky to have survived the beating. It would be a long time before he would recover.

A few weeks later the young man was with a friend. They caught his sister with her lover. He confronted them about their behavior. Robbie, her lover, told the young man he'd do the same to him that Martin had done to Robbie if the young man didn't mind his own business. Robbie laughed as the young man walked away. "I knew you were gutless!" Robbie yelled after him. "You're just like your old man. If he hadn't caught me by surprise, I would've kicked his butt all over the place." The young man just kept walking. Robbie and his sister went back to the truck as if nothing had happened. "Do you think your punk brother will go and get your father?" Robbie asked her.

"No, my brother wouldn't do that. He settles things on his own. Don't underestimate him," she warned.

"What can he do? He's thirteen years old!" About an hour later, a rock hit the side of Robbie's truck breaking his window. Robbie jumped out of the driver's side to confront the vandal.

Tina yelled, "Robbie don't! It's a trap! Get back in the truck. Let's just leave!"

Robbie ignored her pleas and began to chase after the culprit. Just as he came within five feet of the vandal, he suddenly ducked around a corner! As Robbie followed him around the corner he met with a baseball bat swung with full force into his healing ribs. Robbie screamed in agony as blow after blow rained on his injured side. Finally, after what seemed forever, the beating stopped. There was just enough power behind the blow to cause pain, but not enough to make Robbie faint. The assailant knelt down by Robbie's wounded head. Robbie was barely able to open his eyes. He thought he was looking into the face of the young man. But he'd never seen so much hate and fury in a human face before. A voice way too deep and powerful for a thirteen year old bellowed out of him. The young man told Robbie in an icy, calm voice, "This is what I can do about the situation! I don't need to tell my father. I'll gladly kill you myself! This will happen if I ever see you near my sister again!" Then with one final kick to Robbie's side, the young man laughed and walked away.

Two pairs of watchful eyes observed the whole incident. The young man's guides, smiling to them selves, gloated over his actions. They saw him as a warrior becoming worthy of his father's trust. His sister knew what the boy had done and was terrified to say anything. She didn't know what came over her brother when he got angry; it was as if he became another personal altogether. Normally, he was shy and pretty much a loner. Even in the gang, he never really hung out with anyone. He kept mostly to himself. He really wasn't that tough. He definitely wasn't a big person. But when he got mad, it was as if he was the son of the devil, himself! Ever since he was a small child, everyone knew it was best to leave him alone when he became angry. This time he'd gone too far. She confronted the young man and asked him why he couldn't have minded his own business. Why didn't he just walk away? His reaction put the fear of God into her. Responding in a low and very beastly tone, more of a growl then a voice; he replied, "You are a

125

product of the sins of your mother. As she was, so you are. You cannot help your inherited nature. So, therefore; you aren't responsible for your flirtatious actions. On the other hand, Robbie can control himself. Let him go somewhere else and take care of his animalistic needs." Tina was in shock! She couldn't believe her brother had responded so aggressively towards her. When she asked him why, he simply laughed saying, "I didn't label you. You portrayed yourself by your own actions for men to see. Don't complain to me when I identify you by your own actions. Don't try to tell me with words! You have demonstrated who you are by your own actions! Despite your words, your behavior thunders loudly who you are!" With the utterance of these last words, darkness crossed the young man's face and evil filled it. His sister's very blood froze! She no longer dared to talk to him. From that moment on, she began to fear him more then she ever loved him. She finally mustered up the courage to go to her father and tell him what happened. When Martin asked why she was with Robbie, she told him they were talking about the coming baby, and his responsibility to the new baby. Martin said he didn't want Robbie involved with the baby and his brother had simply defended himself against an older man.

23
A LITTLE BIT OF SUNSHINE

"**D**addy!" Tina cried, "Robbie already has broken ribs from the beating you gave him. Butch didn't have to hit him in the ribs with a bat!"

"How was your brother supposed to know Robbie wasn't healed?" Martin asked. "A grown man was chasing him. He was probably so afraid he used the bat to even the odds."

"That's not true!" Tina yelled. "The boy's a lot of things, but afraid isn't one of them. He's totally insane and needs help! You don't even care! If you'd heard him when he was talking to me, you'd know he wasn't himself. He's a devil, Daddy! You need to find him help. One of these days he's going to really lose his temper and kill someone!"

"Oh, stop your foolishness! So he defended himself against that idiot, Robbie. It doesn't make him a killer. You sound like your Aunt Susan. She tried to tell me Butch had a devil living in him. She spends too much time with that moron of a priest. He fills her head with silliness. There's nothing wrong with your brother. If he doesn't learn to defend himself in this world, they'll eat him alive! Now, let me tell you, if I catch Robbie anywhere near you, he won't have to worry about your brother. I'll personally end his problem. Am I clearly understood?"

"Yes, Daddy."

"Good. Now go out and leave me alone!" A few months after
the incident took place, the young man's father woke him up.
"Butch, wake up! You're an uncle! Tina gave birth to a baby
girl! Her name is Karen and she'll be coming home in a couple
of days. You're going to have to help out when she comes
home. She'll need to be diapered and fed. That'll be your
responsibility until Tina can get herself together."

"Dad, I don't know anything about diapering a baby or feeding
it! What if I do something wrong and she gets hurt some how?"

"You don't have to worry about that. She's little but she won't
break. I guarantee it. I'll show you how to feed and diaper her.
Remember, Butch, she's your little niece and she needs you.
Especially since she doesn't have a father around."

"Dad, I already do all of the laundry and the shopping. I go to
school and I work. Why do I have to take care of a baby?"

He replied, "Because I told you she's family. That's all there is
to it. You need to know how to be a father, anyway. You may
as well start now." In a few days the baby came home. In no
time she'd won her uncle's heart. He didn't mind diapering her,
feeding her and taking her for a walk. For the first time he had
someone who was completely dependent on him. She seemed
to love him! It made his day when someone would refer to him
as a good uncle. Everything was going good. The young man
stayed mostly out of trouble. Except for two fights when he
overheard a couple of people talking about his sister and the
situation she was in.

Outside of that, the only other negative incident occurred when
his stepmother came to see the baby. She made a big deal over
the infant. She took his sister out to buy everything the little
one needed. When he refused to talk to her, his father gave him
one of the worse beatings the young man ever received. He left
him lying in his own blood! The hurt inside was harder to bear

than any beating. He was ripped apart inside when he heard his father agree with his stepmother. She complained about how rude he was. He didn't even know how to show proper respect to his elders. What truly hurt the most was his father's response when the stepmother told his father, "Martin, you know he's not all there. Can you trust him around the boy? Aren't you at least a little afraid he might hurt her?" Martin crushed the boy's heart when he coldly said, "Debra, I'll kill him before I let him hurt her!"

The physical pain would disappear, but not the emotional wound he'd just received from the mouth of his own father. He didn't mind everyone thinking he was a mental case. But to think his father thought he might hurt his little niece was more pain than he could bear. This wound would take a miracle to recover from. In the young man's world, miracles didn't happen. From that day on the young man shut everyone out of his heart. He barely spoke to his father again. Hardly a word was said until after he was discharged from the navy. He never did talk to his stepmother again. When she passed away a year later, not even his father's threats could make him go to the funeral. Time passed. The baby was a year old. His sister had her own apartment and both sisters moved out of their father's house. The young man was alone with his father. Things in the projects were going crazy. The gang, as large as ever, was coming under the influence of another spirit and the manifestation was drugs! Most of the members were already high, drunk or trying to find a way to get there.

24
WORDS OF LOVE

The young man was under strict orders from his guides. No drugs! He did drink for a while. An appearance of his spiritual father, Shiva, put an end to that. He told the young man to train his body through rigid exercise. He must leave all drugs and alcohol to the weak and foolish. He was being trained for leadership. By no means was he ever to bring embarrassment to Shiva or his kingdom! The young man willfully obeyed.

Two incidents happened during the summer vacation of his fifteenth year. First, the gang was involved in a turf war over a very popular hangout area in the park in the city of Staunton. The young man had just taken a knife off of the rival gang leader. The war was about to come to an end. As everybody was gathering together to celebrate, treachery struck! One of his own members, under the pretense of congratulating him on the victory, stabbed him twice in the stomach with a switchblade! Someone or something protected the young man that day. The knife didn't go in far. The assistant leader helped him to his feet. The other members beat the traitor into unconsciousness. The young man thought about this. How many more gang wars could he survive? When his time came, would it be at the hands of an enemy or a so-called friend?

The second incident happened a few nights later. The young man was standing on the corner with the gang. A car stopped directly across the street from them. An older black woman got out and approached the young man. When she came near to him she called the young man by his name. She asked the young man if he remembered her. "Yes." he replied. "You're that nut who thinks you're my mother. Hey, if you are my mother, don't you know you've been dead for thirteen years?"

"Young man, don't you speak to me in that tone of voice! You might have these people fooled. You might think you're tough; but I'm not afraid of you!"

"Listen Lady! Why are you bothering me? I didn't ask you to come here. So get out while you can!"

"Don't you threaten me young man! Whether you like it or not, I'm as much your mother as your mother was. You were given into my care for a season. I claimed you for the Lord when you were little. I haven't stopped praying for you since the day your father took you back."

"Lady, you're a nut. Get out of here!"

"Not until you answer a question," she replied.

"What question, Lady?"

"Do you know Jesus?" she asked.

"Jesus! Who?" snapped the young man. "There's no Jesus here, lady. Look around. What would He be doing in hell's kitchen? Go to the freaking Spanish section; everybody's called Jesus there. Maybe that's where you'll find Him. Now lady, I'm not going to tell you again. Leave me alone and get out! If you don't, I'll turn you over to these guys here! And when they're done I'll cut your freaking throat ear to ear!" One of the members of the gang started to come closer. Suddenly, the driver's door of the car opened and the largest human the young man had ever seen emerged. He seemed to cross the street in two steps. The young man and the whole gang couldn't believe the size of this man. When the young man and the gang locked eyes with the giant the young man knew he didn't stand a chance. Something about this person told him he knew everything about the streets. He'd fought and won his share of battles. This was war! The gang couldn't loose face on their turf. Someone was going to be hurt. The overwhelming numbers of the members would guarantee the gang's victory. A strange thought came to the mind of the young man. He thought to himself, this must be what it feels like when a pack of hyenas come face to face with a large lion. Although they may vastly out number him, they still respect and fear his power. The giant stepped between the woman and the young man. There was no trace of fear in the man's voice as he spoke. Everyone knew this was a warrior and he'd give no ground. Neither the large man nor the gang would back off! Just when it looked like violence was inevitable. Just when it looked like no way out, a familiar voice spoke from behind the young man. "James, what are you doing here?"

"Hello Martin. Beatrice and I were visiting church members nearby when Beatrice spotted your son. She came over to talk to him. I stayed in the car until these fellows started surrounding Beatrice. Then I figured I'd come over to see if there was some kind of misunderstanding."

"Boys, this is a friend of mine and his wife. Now I'll tell you. This man is a legend. I know you don't want any part of him, but if you come against him you come against me!" Martin walked over and stood at the side of the giant. His head came up to the shoulder of the man. The members knew Martin and there was no way they'd challenge him. Never mind trying to take on the giant as well. To make matters worse. The rear doors of the car opened and two more huge men got out. They crossed over and stood by the woman. "Martin, these two young men are our nephews. They came to live with us right after you came back for the boy."

"James." Martin laughed, "With these two monsters, I don't think you need my help."

"Well, Martin," said James, "you know we have to watch our words. Words are powerful. *There is life and death in our tongue.* Jesus warned us not to speak idle words or destructive words. These men are big, but they're not monsters. In fact, Beatrice and I consider them angels. They're real blessings sent by God to help us in our old age."

"James," said Martin, "you're still preaching. Maybe I'm an angel sent by God tonight to stop some unnecessary bloodshed. What do you think, James? Think your God could use the likes of me?"

James replied with a smile, "Martin, you know God used a jackass in the Old Testament to warn a prophet!"

Martin laughed, "Who's the prophet and who's the jackass here, James?" defusing the situation. Even the gang members began to laugh.

"James." said Martin, "I don't know if you called me a name or you're just telling me God can even work through a thick headed Irishman like me. I wish you luck with your religion, but if I were you, I wouldn't waste my time on the likes of these. They're nothing but a bunch of sinners and street trash. And that goes double for my kid!"

"Well Martin," replied James. "I'm sure you learned from your mom and dad. They were good folks. *Christ came for the sinner and the lost!* He came for this street trash as you called them, not for the righteous. The righteouses don't need a doctor. It's the sick who need healing."

"James," answered Martin, "I know better than to argue with you. But your religion won't save you on these streets. You're a warhorse and a lion, James. I know you. I remember the legend of you. I remember who you were. But even a lion, as strong as he is, can be taken down by a pack of hyenas."

"Martin," proclaimed James, "you're right! Religion will not save me on these streets. But my faith in Jesus will! Martin, here's my card. We live right here in town. We have a small church. You're welcome; as are all your friends. Come by at any time. Feel free to call if you need prayer."

Beatrice poked her head out from behind James and spoke directly to the young man. "Butch, I'm a mother to you. I don't care if you cut my throat. With my dying breath I'll tell you – I love you and Jesus does too."

"Lady, Shut Up!" shouted Butch. "I don't want to hear any more garbage about your make-believe Jesus. You stay away from me. Stay away from here. I rule here and I don't want you to spreading your nutcase fanaticism around here. We have enough problems. We don't need any more!"

Martin heard enough, "Butch, watch your mouth! You might be in charge of this ragged bunch of misfits, but I rule you. You're in danger of opening your big mouth once too many times. If you do it again, I'll close it for you!"

"What are you going to do, Dad?" asked Butch." Beat me, again? Big freaking deal! How many times have you done that? One more won't make a difference. You've always told me religion was my choice. I choose not to listen to this junk. So, do I have the right to choose? Or are you going to force me to believe in something you don't?" With one last angry scowl, the young man turned and walked away with the gang trailing after him.

After a moment James and Martin shook hands. James asked him, "Is there anyway I can convince you to return to the faith of your parents?"

Martin just laughed, "James, you are persistent. There's no way. Don't you understand? God wasn't there for me when Mary died all those years ago. He's not here for me now! Mary was all that mattered to me. If your God couldn't save her, I don't need Him. So, James, let's part friends while we still can."

"Ok Martin, but I won't stop praying for you."

"Fair enough James. But understand; you chose to believe. You have that right. I chose not to. That is my right. As far as hell is concerned, why should I worry about that? Can't you see I already live in hell?"

"Martin this is bad, but, seriously, it's not hell! You can't imagine the horror hell will be! Please, reconsider your decision and ask God to come into your life."

"James I told you, I don't need God! He's already taken my wife and my health. I can't even find a job. What more can he take from me? My life? Big deal! My life was over thirteen years ago when Mary died. Good-bye, James. I strongly advise you, don't come back here! There's nothing you can do for these people. All your religion will do is give them false hope with a promise of some pie in the sky, by-and-by. What they really need is bread in their children's stomach right now!"

James and Beatrice just looked sadly as Martin walked away.

"Oh, James," shared Beatrice, "what great potential that man has for leadership. Did you notice how everyone listened when he spoke? Look how easily he disarmed the situation? With just one look – if only he'd give his heart to Jesus. He could be a modern day Paul!"

"Yes Beatrice, but his heart's hardened. He's endured more than he can handle, alone. His pride won't allow him to surrender to Jesus. But Jesus is his only hope! When he lost his wife, he shut out the world. Worse than that; he shut out God! All we can do is pray."

"James! What about the young man? He's so lost. He's already ensnared in his mother's lie. I've never seen so much hatred in a young man. He wasn't even afraid of Martin beating him! It was as if it was a normal way of life. Dear Lord, what has this child been through since he left us?"

"Come on, Beatrice, there is nothing more we can do tonight."

~~ Beatrice's Vow ~~

"Oh, James, I won't stop praying for that young man. Not until he's pulled from the enemy's camp." James walked Beatrice and his two nephews back to their waiting car. Unnoticed by the four warriors of God, a lone figure stood in the dark. His eyes were filled with hate and anger; darkly leering as they got back in the vehicle. "You'll never take this one from me. You miserable lumps of clay! He's mine for all of eternity! You better watch yourself old man; and that meddlesome wife of yours! Be sure you're under the blood at all times. Don't step out! For given the slightest chance, I'll destroy both of you!" Looking up at heaven, the dark figure screamed, "Keep your filthy slaves away from my son, Nazarene! I'll never bow down to you! I rule this mud hole called earth. Someday I'll rule heaven, my rightful home! You'll see the cross was only a temporary setback. I will win! You had your chance, now I'll force you to kneel in front of all creation and worship me!" The master shook his fist at heaven arrogantly bellowing blasphemies at the God of all creation. Suddenly, pain racked his massive body. He felt as if he'd been delivered a mighty blow from an invisible foe. It felt like blow after blow landed unseen on his body. The pain was unbearable. It dawned on him the four warriors of the Nazarene were praying against him. They were using Jesus' name and quoting His Word. The master had to flee. He had lost this battle tonight. But he was determined not to lose the war. The young man and his father were firmly in his grip. "You miss your Mary so much Martin?

Well, you can join her in hell!" he screamed, as he vanished from the presence of the praying saints.

25
ANOTHER INVITATION

The young man and the gang were sitting in their clubhouse. These were two empty apartments they'd claimed for themselves. The warlord spoke up, "Man, those were three of the biggest dudes I've ever seen! The old guy wasn't afraid of anything! Butch, your old man stands six feet five easy. This dude was head and shoulders over him. Man, he must have weighed nearly four hundred pounds. He was rock solid! But that wasn't what bothered me. That dude and his wife reeked with power! I mean, Butch, it was like something just warned you there was just no way you wanted any trouble with these two! Never mind when the twin King Kong's showed up. When they started talking that religious stuff, man, I just wanted to run. I don't know what it is about those two. But I'd liked to receive some of that power! That Jesus cat must be one powerful dude!"

"What do you want to do, Dan?" asked Butch. "Join their church? Did all that freaking religious talk get to you? We both go to church every Sunday. We both listen to the priest. It doesn't do anything for us, does it?"

"That's the difference, Butch," replied Dan. "What those people said did something! It wasn't like the priest. Man, there was power! Not only is their power in them; but also in their words. Look, even your father respected that guy, James. He couldn't argue with him."

"Listen, Dan, there's no God!" shared Butch. "If you want to worship something, worship me! Or shut up about this religious stuff! If my old man didn't intervene, we would've found out just how powerful that old man and his nephews were."

"Well," said Dan. "I for one am glad Martin was there. I have a funny feeling we would've been fighting more than three big men."

"Yea, that's right!" most of the members agreed.

"Well, if you punks are so scared of some old man and some old woman, why don't you go and join his little church? Get out of this gang! We don't need no religious fanatics or Jesus freaks!" said Butch.

The gang replied, "We aren't punking out. We're just stating fact. We didn't see you leap frogging tonight. I saw you size him up. Face it Butch, you can't handle your father, yet.
Never mind that giant. He'd have cleaned your clock if you'd tried to jump him."

Butch said defensively, "Well, at least I was willing to jump! Don't you ever forget it Sammy. Cause you aren't that dude and I'll clean your clock for you right now if you run your mouth any more!"

"Ok, you two." replied one of the gang members. "This fight ain't among us and no one's disrespecting you. Dan's only voicing what a lot of us is feeling right now."

"Say what you want Butch." said another one of the guys, "But that's one battle we would've lost. It was as if God was fighting on his side."

"Carlos," said Butch, "you and your cousin Sammy are '*muy loco*.'"

The young man paused, and then said, "You are right. The fight is not among us. Sorry guys. That old lady freaks me out. This is the second time she's tried to convert me with that religious junk. I agree with my father. I don't need no religion. I don't believe there's a God who cares. I don't believe 'cause my life wouldn't be so messed up. I wouldn't have to be hanging around with you bunch of ugly apes!"

"Hey!" yelled the guys, "Look who's calling ugly ugly."

They all laughed.

"Hey!" said one of the guys, "We can start our own religion!"

"Yea, Butch. You can be like the devil. You know. The rebellious leader. We'll be your fallen angels." Once more, everyone laughed. They began to separate and to go home. For a long time after everyone left the young man sat in the empty apartment alone, thinking. Why wouldn't that crazy lady leave him alone? What was this junk about her raising him and loving him? Nobody ever loved him but his grandfather. This lady wanted him to believe that not only did she love him, but God loved him too! Yeah, right. God loved him so much that He made him a cripple. He took his mother. Let him live with Debra and experience five years of hell on earth. He took his father's health so he couldn't work any more. He put him in this hellhole they call home. And to top all it off! He took his grandfather, the only person who truly made life worth living. Yeah, God loved him. He sure had a funny way of showing it. The young man looked towards heaven and yelled, "Hey, God! If you're listening, as the old woman said, then hear this! Quit loving me! I can't stand the freakin pain! There's nothing more for me to lose!" Once again a dark shadow moved unnoticed in the darkness. With an unholy laugh he snarled. "This is one you'll never have, Nazarene. His soul is mine! With all the pain in his life, no one will ever convince him you care."

~~ A New Season ~~

The summer passed without any further incident. The school year started and, as usual, the young man felt out of place. Most of the classes bored him to tears. He didn't get along with any of the students; because he came from the projects. None of the teachers expected him to get involved in any of the class activities. In fact, the Latin teacher made a deal with him. If he didn't disturb the class, he'd give him a D+ so he could pass the class! Butch and the teacher didn't get along; so he agreed to the offer. He didn't know why the guidance counselor wanted him to take Latin in the first place. He couldn't even speak English correctly! The meningitis, that almost killed him as an infant, so damaged his vocal cords, it made speaking very difficult. He just came to school so he wouldn't have to stay home. To top it all off, he was getting harassed by some of the jocks in class!

One day, after school, he went to confront one of them. But he walked into a trap! Three pairs of brass knuckles and a bat proved more than a match for him. He still managed to put one of his opponent's head through a car window. The young man had a broken jaw and most of his upper teeth were knocked out. He placed his foot firmly between the legs of a second opponent. This made it possible for him to escape before any further damage was done. A couple of days later, he returned to school to the stares and gossip of his fellow students. Although he'd gotten the worst part of beatings, he'd earned respect among the jocks and they weren't willing to continue the war. Victory against the young man was too costly. But, for the first time in seven years, the gang failed him. When he made it to the safety of the projects, most of the guys were stoned out of their heads. It was getting to be a constant thing with them. Lately, they were always strung out. Drugs did to them what no other gang could do. The once feared Hell's Kitchen gang was now nothing more than a bunch of drug addicts. These warriors no longer had the energy to fight their way out of a paper bag. Most of the members were so concerned about their next high they couldn't concentrate on anything else. Some were in jail or youth detention hall. Life was changing for everyone. After three more months of school, Butch got a job and quit school. His father didn't even know, until a month later, when Butch finally told him. All Martin asked was, "Are you sure you want to do this?"

One night, about a month after he told his father he'd quit school, his guides once again appeared to him. Butch asked them where they were on the day he'd been beaten so badly. Weren't they supposed to be there to make sure no harm came to him? The guides told him that, sometimes, he had to be allowed to suffer things to understand the seriousness of life and the important value of the master's help. Without the master's help he'd always be a victim. Hadn't he learned that no one could be trusted? Not even those who were closest to him? Anyone could and would betray him for whatever reason appealed to them. The only thing that would bring him peace was to serve the master faithfully. Then he'd be rewarded. Butch now burst out to the guides and said, "So when do I receive some rewards? So far, in this life, I've lost my mother, my grandfather, the ability to speak right or walk normally. My father lost his health and we have to live in absolute poverty. Now I have my jaw broken and my upper teeth knocked out! Is this the reward for being faithful to the master? You can keep your blessings! I don't need them or you! It seems as though all my freaking life people have been telling me what to do and when to do it! I think it's time for me to live my own life!"

"You'd better be careful with your smart attitude young man. The master's been more than patient with you. He owes you no explanation for anything he does. He is Lord and cannot be challenged. Those who are foolish enough to do so will pay for their insolence. That includes you!"

"Know what? Threats don't mean anything to me. My stepmother used to threaten me when I lived with her. The gang threatened me. My father threatens me all the freaking time! Even you, oh great Ola, spirit of the dead, have

143

threatened me. Well, I just don't care. Destroy me if you want. You've already made my life a living hell!"

"You say I'm the son of the master. Big Deal! He treats me no different than my father. All I am to Martin is an errand boy and a whipping post! I don't see the master treating me any better. Let the master choose another boy to take my place. He can have all my so-called blessings!"

The master interrupted as he instantly appeared shouting, "What's the meaning of all this complaining and murmuring? One little trial! One simple little test and you, who are meant to be a prince and ruler in my kingdom; fall a part!"

"You want out? No warrior can ever be promoted to an officer, to a ruler of any army; until their loyalty has been proven by fire. Boy, don't be in such a big hurry to go to hell! Once you're there, there's no leaving!" bellowed the master! Chango and Ola quickly bowed to show their respect. The young man just stood there with his eyes locked on to the master's face.

"I don't expect to leave hell when I get there." said Butch." I just don't expect to live in hell while I am here! The testing and trials I can handle. I don't mind you testing me. As I told you before, my life is yours. What troubles me is you can never be honest with me. You aren't up front with me. If getting my jaw broken and my teeth knocked out proves something to you, fine! If it's absolutely necessary for your master plan for your kingdom then, fine! Just let me know. Don't leave me in the dark all the time. I'm not a child anymore. I don't need to be locked in a closet to obey. Just tell me what you want and I'll do my best to please you. Is that too much to ask?"

"No, it's not. I'll explain my purpose to you when I feel it's necessary. I told you before; you're a prince, not the king! You may think it's necessary for me to tell you everything. I don't. As long as I'm king, I'll make the rules. Is that clear? Be very careful how you dare to challenge me. For another day may not find me as merciful as I am today. I may grant your wish. You will join your mother soon enough. Not for a short time but forever! Don't hasten your fate. Am I clear, young man?" Butch just stared, not wanting to give in. But he knew he'd lost the battle. He was lucky to have kept his life! His anger and frustration were leaving. He realized how foolish he was acting. Challenging the master like he had could've been tortuously fatal. He'd have to be satisfied that the master had appeared and spoken to him. The young man looked once more into the master's face, bowed his head and bent his knee showing the master the respect he craved.

"Once again, I apologize for my rudeness. I know better than to let my emotions rule my mind. My life is always yours to do with as you please. You are lord and master. I am your servant. It's not for me to question you. It is only for me to obey. No matter what! I'm just so angry over what happened. The gang was useless! I've learned not to trust anyone! For all are capable of betraying if the situation favors them."

"Now you're beginning to understand." Sneered his master. "You're proving your loyalty, but remember your own words. Everyone can be a traitor if the situation favors it. That includes you as well!"

"Where would I go? Who could I trust if I betrayed you? Who would trust me? If my actions don't prove my loyalty, neither will my promise of loyalty prove it."

"You are wise, young man. You please me. Yes, a man's actions can speak so loud one would be deaf to his words. It's a good thing when actions and words agree as one. So far, your words serve only to confirm what your deeds have already loudly spoken. Notice, I'm aware of the damage to you and those who have done it. They shall pay dearly for it! We don't turn the other cheek as our enemy does. Instead, we strike the other cheek hard and repeatedly! How can people learn if you don't teach them? How will they ever know if we let things go? Now go and continue your studies. Learn more of me. I will speak to you again." Butch knew he was fortunate. The master hadn't lashed out at him or punished him for his rebellious attitude. He knew his biggest weakness was his temper and his inability to control it. He may be able to get away with loosing it with men; but it could cost him his life with the master. He'd be sure to never show that much disrespect ever again! In spite of all his weaknesses and shortcomings, being stupid wasn't one of them. Life taught him, at an early age that you can't win every battle. It was important to know when to retreat and not fight. As time went on, his guides began to train him and draw him deeper into the arts and meditations. He was quickly able to get in touch with his god-consciousness and to astral-project his spirit at will! The older members of the covens were always trying to teach him new magic, rites and spells; as well as counter-spells. He thought this was mostly nonsense. Why does he have to use all this foolishness when he can speak to his guides or the master directly? He brought his requests to pass without all this ritual!

His guides explained it to him. Not all members of the covens are as developed as he is. They don't have the privilege of being the son of Shiva. They aren't able to communicate directly with Shiva as the young man can. Even the most highly developed among them can only communicate with the master after great effort on their part. The master doesn't appear to every one. He isn't simply at their beck and call. After all, he is their master, not their servant! It is his choice as to whom he shows himself to, not theirs. The master will only show himself to those who are completely loyal and faithful to him. He will show himself only to those who follow every rule and instruction. Many boast about being able to communicate with their guides and even channeled spirits! But few can say they've actually seen the master in all of his splendor and glory. Oh yes, there are many who claimed to have seen him. They are usually those who are strung out on drugs and spent hours talking to rocks and trees. These pitiful fools are mistaking their shadows for spirits or even the master himself! Unlike them, the young man can talk with the master because of his relationship. He is the chosen vessel! By virtue of his relationship, he can by pass all their religious rituals and ceremonies when he is alone. Yet, at the gatherings, when others are around, it is necessary for him to show proper respect. If he, the son of Shiva, doesn't do so, why should anyone else?

26
NEED FOR DISCIPLINE

Now, the young man can see how easily this could cause things to get out of hand. Without orders and rules there'd be no control! Everything would fall apart. He understood the followers of the master were self-centered, lazy and very undisciplined. They will, by their rebellious nature, seek the easiest way around all activities. The least amount of work they have to do, the better. They preferred to have someone else to do the work while they enjoy the benefits. Butch knows there are some in the inner circle who would gladly kill him. They lust to take his place if it's possible. Already, at this early age, he has to defend himself against powerful psychic attacks! Attacks from those who truly believed the master will let them take the young man's place. If they can only defeat him in an open, spiritual battle! He remembered an assault that came when he was only six years old. He lay in his bed for two weeks. His fever went as high as 106 degrees before one of the watchers came to his aid and successfully turned the psychic assault back upon his attackers!

From that time on, his watchers and guides made sure he paid close attention to counter-spells and charms of protection. No one will ever come close enough to attack him like that; ever again! What troubled him the most during the assaults and time of sickness was no one even bothered to check him. His father would come in once in the morning before work and once at night when he came home. He gave him medicine and fluid and he always told his grandparents the same thing. 'He's ok. He'll make it. He's strong. Don't need to worry about him. Just let him lie in bed. He'll come out when he's ready.' His grandfather asked his son, "Shouldn't you call a doctor?"

He'd always reply, "There's no need for any doctor. I've got vapor rub, cough medicine, and aspirin. He'll make it on his own. There's no use in spoiling or babying him. The boy needs to fight, if he's going to be strong and make it in this world. If he doesn't, with the handicap he has, perhaps he'd be better off if he doesn't make it." His grandparents were under strict orders not to go in and baby him. Martin said if they did, he'd become lazy and want to spend time in bed. Butch was trained from an early age, to rule and reign by the master's side. As time went by he grew into that calling spiritually, emotionally and physically. He trained himself spiritually, by the studies of all occult science and religions, except that of the followers of the Jew called Jesus. Mentally, he conditioned himself to never show his emotions. No matter what! He was always in complete control of his feelings. Physically, he reached a point where he could do 300 push ups, non-stop! He could military press 300 pounds at the body weight of 130! He went on to earn two black belts. He was an undefeated fighter in the pits!

~~ The separation ~~

The time came when he began to separate from the gang and all of his former associates. He just went to work and came home, studied and worked out. He no longer needed the gang. Most of them had already ruined their lives and many of the others would have no future. Most of those who didn't die from violence would die from drug abuse. Many of the rest would spend what little life they had in prison or mental institutions.

27
A WAY OUT - SHIPS AHOY!

One day, while the young man was going to pick up his check, a Navy recruiter approached him. His office was across the hall from the young man's place of employment. The recruiter stopped him and asked what he was planning to do with his life. Butch, at the age of seventeen, is seeking a new life. But where could he begin? Where should he go to make this happen? His father certainly didn't teach him a trade or guide him into a career choice. It was no coincidence the recruiter approached Butch that day. The recruiter simply asked if he'd be interested in joining the Navy. He shared some of the benefits of service. Butch replied, "I don't know, man. I don't have much of a life and there's not much I can do with the little I have." The recruiter, who introduced himself as Chief Petty Officer Dan Baker, asked if he'd be interested in giving the Navy a chance. Butch replied, "The Navy wouldn't want me. I am a high school drop out and I'm only seventeen."

Chief Baker said, "It's ok. If you're interested, and your father will sign the papers, you can get in on a special program the Navy calls the 'Kiddy Cruise.'" Butch, for the first time in his life, sensed this stranger was actually trying to give him a way out. He was really interested in him as a person and not just a number. He told the Chief he'd think about it and talk to his father. He'd be back to him in a few days. In a week's time,

Butch returned to begin one of the many serious talks he'd have over the next two months with Chief Baker. Finally, one day in March, he came back with the signed papers. He was on his way to Boston to take the test. He had to fail the test in order to meet the requirements. One of the conditions of the 'Kiddy Cruise!' He took the test. He placed highest in his class of recruits! When he returned, Chief Baker remarked, "What are you trying to do?"

Butch was confused and asked, "What do you mean, sir?"

Chief Baker stated, "Didn't I mention you needed to *fail* the written exam in order to qualify to get in on the special deal?"

"Yes, sir, you did."

"Well, you didn't! You placed right on top of the list! You need to go back. Retake the test and fail. You must understand or the deal is off. You don't need to end up in the Army. In a few months, you'll be drafted into this bloody Vietnam crisis. You don't need that. Please listen to me! Go back and fail that test! Ok?"

"Yes sir, Chief Baker! I'll just pretend I'm back in Latin class and put down any answers to the questions." Butch went back and failed. Shortly after he turned eighteen, he found himself in boot camp training to become a sailor. Boot camp wasn't all that bad. He heard rumors about how tough it would be and how some wouldn't qualify. He knew he had to keep his mouth shut and do what he was told. Then he'd make it. The physical part was no problem. He was in good condition. He could hold his own. The mental part wasn't too tough either. For the first time in his life, he actually felt he had a good mind and he needed to use it. The Navy wouldn't tolerate a slacker. A slacker was someone who refused to do his best and just skated by on everyone else's effort. He placed fifth out of 1,500 recruits after taking the General Education Diploma test. His commanding officers were absolutely amazed. They chewed him out for wasting the brain God had given him. He just laughed and stated, "Sir, the only thing God ever gave me was trouble. I don't expect him to give me anything now. There's no God who helps people. Nothing's ever given freely without a catch."

"Sir, I learned a long time ago, I'm the only one who's responsible for my life. I don't expect a handout from God or from the Navy. As a matter of fact, everything I'll receive in life or in the service I'll receive 'cause I earned it! If I don't earn it, I don't want it!"

"Well, Seaman Recruit Louis, that attitude will hurt your naval career and your chances for advancement!"

"Sir, I'm not looking for a career in the Navy. I owe my country six years of military duty and I'll pay what I owe. I'm free after that. Free from any obligation. As far as promotions and advancements are concerned; if I can't pass the tests and assignments, then I don't deserve them. If I do pass them, they'll be mine."

"Young man, I don't understand why you're so angry. I don't understand why you look at the world the way you do. But, can't you see this is your opportunity to leave your old ways behind? Everything that troubled you in the past can be left behind; once and for all. A new life can be yours!"

"Sir, I can no more walk away from yesterday than I can from this camp. Even if I manage to get through the gates, eventually, the Navy will find me and bring me back. I'll face the brig. It's that way with my life. One who is far greater than the Navy will find me if I try to leave. The prison I'll face will be eternal!"

"Young man, don't you know there's a God who cares and loves you? He can protect you from anything!"

"Sir, I have experienced the care of your so-called loving God. It was your loving God who took my mother at the age of twenty-two. It was the same loving God who caused me to suffer from meningitis as an infant. He left me unable to walk or talk for years. It was your loving God who placed me in the hands of a jealous, mentally unstable stepmother. She tormented me day and night for over five years! She nearly took my life on more than one occasion. It was the same God who placed me in the Ghetto. He took my father's health and his peace of mind. It was the so-called God of compassion who stood by as my father, in order to vent out his frustrations; repeatedly beat me until he was too exhausted to lift his arms to continue. It was this God of understanding who took the only source of love in my life, my grandfather, so I'd have no one to trust in. Sir, you can keep your God! I don't think I can survive any more of His blessings."

"Young man, I'll pray for you. Life's obviously been very difficult for you, but you can't blame God! It wasn't God who dealt you this. But you don't understand."

"Understand what, sir? You told me your God is all-powerful. So, who else can I blame? If He's so powerful, He doesn't need me. I've endured His so-called mercy and grace from His hands. I don't want Him! I don't need Him!" Try as hard as the commanding officer of the base could, the old man couldn't get through the hardened heart of this young recruit. The more he tried to share the love of God with the new recruit, the more the young man rejected Him. He was a strange lad. He obeyed orders and worked well with his platoon. He didn't give anyone any trouble, but was definitely a loner. He cared for his country and loved his family. There was coldness in his eyes, which almost seemed supernatural. His calm exterior concealed within a raging storm. The young man had actually been sent to *Special Forces training*. Not once, but twice! Butch had a serious varicose vein problem in his left leg. He was forced to be released from the program.   That disappointed his commanding officer. He truly felt the young man had all the makings of a top-notch **Special Forces** member. He finally graduated from boot camp and received his orders to report to Norfolk, Virginia for duty. After two weeks leave the young man reported to his ship. He'd barely arrived on board ship when he was in a fistfight with the Petty Officer of the deck. Word got out about this young hot head. He was escorted to the berthing area and given a rack and a locker. Two friends of the Petty Officer came down to check him out. He was not aboard ship for an hour before he was involved in two more fights.

He was brought before the Chief Petty Officer for trial. He made it clear he wouldn't be pushed around or ordered about by punks. No matter what their ranks were! The Chief made it clear he'd follow orders from anyone who outranked him. He was restricted to the ship for ten days. His only reply was, "I don't care! There isn't anywhere in this state I want to be, anyway." The Chief asked him what his position was. The young man told him he was supposed to be the new ship's barber. The three Petty Officers and Chief broke out in laughter. The Chief didn't think that a hot head like the young man could be trusted with scissors and a straight razor. The Chief demoted him to work on deck. He was a deck ape. The trial ended. The three Petty Officers came up to the young man. The four were able to put the incident aside and become friends. They actually did all they could to help him with his temper. He'd learn his lessons through ten fights and being busted two times for losing his temper.

It looked like he'd be given a general discharge if he didn't exercise a little more self-control. When he heard the news it deeply troubled him. It meant he'd be a failure. His father and all of his uncles received honorable discharges. One of his uncles had given his life for his country in World War II, as a Special Force Ranger. He didn't want people to think he couldn't make it. As soon as he could, he asked for permission to see the Captain. He was granted his meeting. He apologized for being a troublemaker and asked for a second chance. The Captain granted it and the young man made a complete turn around! He stopped drinking and began going to the gym. He worked out in the boxing ring where he earned a good reputation.

One night he was celebrating with his shipmates. One of his buddies was celebrating his birthday and the other his advancement in rank. The effects of drinking made him return to the ship before he got in trouble. He gave his word. He'd never drink again. He only had one more chance. He'd been asleep for about an hour when he was awakened by a fellow shipmate who'd mistaken him for someone else. Jumping angrily out of the rack, he began to push and threaten the other sailor. The man tried to apologize for the mistake. But Butch was too drunk to listen. What happened next caught him totally off guard. He began to throw punches at his shipmate. The fellow easily blocked all of his punches. To add insult to injury, he pinned his arms to his side! "Hey, man. My name is Curtis. I didn't mean any harm. Please, believe me. I apologize. I didn't mean to wake you. I thought this was Harris's rack. You're in no condition to fight tonight. So in the morning, when you sober up, if you want to continue this; we can go on the fantail of the ship. Until then…good night!"

Curtis released him and simply turned and walked away; without even looking back!

"Ok tough guy." Butch muttered. The young man knew Curtis was right. "I'm too drunk to fight. We'll see what the morning brings."

In the morning, after he showered, shaved and dressed, he went to the fantail where he was met by Curtis and a man called Harris. In the light of the morning, the events of the previous evening didn't seem so important. But he still had to prove to this guy he was no push over. Curtis immediately took control and apologized once again for the mistake, defusing the need for violence. Butch and Curtis talked for a while. The young man's respect for Curtis soon developed. Butch found out Curtis had a black belt, both in Karate and Judo. He was working for another belt in a different style. Curtis wrestled and boxed in high school and college. That's why he could so effortlessly block the drunken punches thrown at him the night before. The two became close friends. Before long Butch noticed Curtis never seemed to become angry or swear. He'd never back down from trouble. He always seemed to be able to defuse the situation without resorting to violence. Butch asked Curtis what his secret was. He replied, "The presence of the Lord within me. He provides the answer to every situation in my life. He gives me the authority to accept things and remain in control of myself."

"What Lord is this?" Butch asked. "The lord of my life seems to bring all problems and no solution."

"Why, it's the Lord Jesus Christ!" Curtis stated. "Don't you know about Him?"

"If you mean the Jew they crucified so many years ago. Yea, I've heard of Him. But no, I don't know Him and He doesn't know me."

"You're wrong!" Curtis said. "You may not know Him, but He knows you. *He knew you even before the foundation of the earth!* He knew you before He formed you in your mother's belly. God is the Creator of all men and therefore their Father."

"No, Curtis." Butch replied. "God isn't my Father. I will not accept that! My father is the lord of this world. He gave me life and he can take that back anytime he wants too, just as he did to my mother. As far as your Jesus is concerned, He's but a character in a Jewish fable. Just like all the religions. They have their stories and the Jews have theirs.

In fact, He was a Jew and the Jews didn't even believe in Him! To tell you the truth, after being forced to attend my mother's church, they still managed to remove all reverence for your so-called Messiah. In fact, He's still nailed to the cross in all their churches! Every time the service is performed, He's crucified again and again. If He can't deliver Himself from torment on a cross, how can He help and deliver others?"

"Well, Butch, I've never heard so much anger and bitterness from someone so young before. Do you truly believe what you just said is absolute truth?"

"Yes I do, Curtis, with everything I have. The suffering I've gone through has brought me to this point. God truly cares for no one but Himself! I don't see evidence of His Son taking my place."

~ The Invitation ~

"Butch, would you be willing to come with me for a home cooked meal this weekend? You could meet my sister and attend church? I believe you'll find your answers there."

"I don't mind going home with you and meeting your sister. But I'm not sure about church. If I go somewhere without my father's permission; it will cost me dearly."

"Butch, you're in the Navy. What can your Dad do to you?"

"Curtis, you don't understand. It's not Martin I'm talking about. I'll get back to you. I promise."

Later that night, Butch called forth Ola and Chango, his spirit guides. It had been a while since his last meeting with them. The two appeared. He quickly filled them in on everything that happened since the last meeting. He was surprised and caught off guard when he was told Shiva approved of him going to the church with Curtis over the weekend.

Butch asked, "Why would Shiva give permission to go to a church that honored the Jew called Jesus?"

Chango simply said, "Shiva doesn't fear the power of the Jewish carpenter. This church will teach the truth and curiosity will be once and for all done away with!" The weekend found Butch in a place where he'd never been before. It was a Protestant Church. This was the place where the Words of the

Nazarene and the Jewish Messiah were quoted. He didn't understand any of the songs or what the sermon was about. The preacher reminded him of a slick used car salesman. But because he valued Curtis' friendship, he agreed to come back.

28
NEW CHURCH EXPERIENCE

After he returned to the ship, he was standing watch on the fantail when Ola, spirit of the dead, appeared. He was surprised to see him without Chango. So he asked why Ola appeared alone. The guide replied, "I am here by the master's request. What knowledge have you gleaned from attending the house of Jewish Carpenter?"

∼ Couldn't Understand? ∼

The young man replied, "Nothing! I couldn't understand the songs. All of them seemed so depressing; all about enduring trials and tribulations. They were pleading blessings from heaven and begging for mercy to endure the hardship of life, which comes their way. By their songs and their prayers they appeared to have no joy or victory. The sermon seemed to condemn anyone who didn't agree with the preacher's way of thinking. There was more talk about money than about the God they supposedly believe in. I came away more confused than before I went! The man at the church told me I was evil and a sinner. He said I was God's enemy and had broken the law. What law was he speaking about? Who made the law? Why was I God's enemy? What have I done? I didn't ask to be created and put in this world. Why should I be blamed for the sins of Adam and Eve and everyone else? Why should I be forced to take the blame for everyone else's mistakes? So many questions and no answers! Curtis didn't have any time to talk to me. He seemed to be impatient with me because I didn't just lie down and accept everything I was told. They both seemed more interested in telling me how wrong I was for believing what I was taught all my life! And how right they were to believe what they were taught to believe all their lives. I guess all I came away knowing is that everyone who disagrees with what they teach to be truth is wrong and going to hell. I definitely didn't feel any love and they truly wanted me to be apart of their religious circle or club. If their God is love; why are His people so cold hearted? I don't understand."

"Now, you see the wisdom of your father, Shiva? Why he told you to go? You needed to see this for yourself. Now, I'm here to tell you, at his request, to continue to attend until further notice. You'll know when the time is up." Ola told him the master was pleased with the young man's open mindedness and his development. He said his time in the Navy will be soon over and he can, once again, continue his deep training. He must expand his father's kingdom! The boy thanked Ola and told him to tell his father he obeys him in all things. Ola told the young man he was pleased he'd learned to control his temper and to submit to authority. He also reminded him to keep away from alcohol and from relationships with women. He must continue his physical training. After the meeting with Ola, the ship pulled out for a short trip and the events of the church service were forgotten. When the cruise was over and the ship returned to port, Curtis invited the young man to go home with him, once again. Butch readily agreed and went back to the church in Ohio.

The service was just like the previous one. All he got from those services was he was no good. God hated him and he was on his way to hell. He was hopeless and there wasn't anything he could do about it. He was born in sin and would die in sin, spending eternity in hell. All because God, who made him, hated him and condemned him since birth. Those who were saved seemed to be the most wretched creatures around. They were never happy, always fearful and bitter. And man! You should hear the women of the church gossip! The old men constantly made bets on how long it would be before the new converts would backslide whenever someone would go forward, as they called it. The members of this church had the young man convinced he couldn't be saved and if he did he couldn't stay saved. Somehow, in spite of all the negative deeds and words; Butch continued to go to the little church.

~~ Butch and the little church ~~

One Sunday, the young man was really acting up in the back of the church. He was teasing two sisters who were trying to listen to the sermon. He felt a hand grab him by the back of his neck and yank him to his feet. Before he knew what was happening he was halfway down the isle! He couldn't stop and with every step forward his rage was welling up inside. He just knew it had to be the grip of one of those two giant ushers. These two ushers were ex-wrestlers. They'd resigned from the World Wrestling Association and became Christians. These two wrestlers wouldn't tolerate any disrespect in the church. Well, no matter how big they were, they had no right to make a public spectacle of him in front of the whole church! He fought all the way down. He was about three quarters of the way down the isle before he realized no one was behind him! It was like some mysterious force had him by the neck! When that realization hit him, he knew it had to be a power beyond man! Something supernatural!

The next thing he knew, he was on his knees at the altar. For over two hours he wept. He gave his heart to a God he didn't know or understand. He was consumed with grief for the wrongs he'd done. He wasn't just grieving over the consequences his sins and selfish actions had wrought; he actually began to hate the sins! He was experiencing true repentance! During the two hours he remained on his knees. But, no one came to him or touched him or encouraged him. The people were busy with two others who'd come to the altar. They were family members of the congregation. He was a stranger. They assumed, surely, the newly converted family members would remain saved while the stranger would probably just backslide in a few days. When he stood, there were no hugs or congratulations like the others received. What he received was a stern word from the pastor of the church. He told him God didn't appreciate game players. He'd be watching to see just how serious the young man was. It seemed the preacher didn't believe him or even want him to be saved! It didn't matter.

For the first time in his life he felt great! He'd been accepted and forgiven by the Most High God! That night at supper, Curtis's mother gave the young man a Bible as a gift and asked him to read it. Butch took it and began to devour every word! Every free moment was spent reading it. Every time he saw Curtis he had new questions. When he went to church, he asked the preacher some questions. The constant barrages of questions were overwhelming to the preacher. He'd turn and go the other way, if Curtis saw him coming first. Butch didn't care. He was truly happy. He had the little Bible he read so much. Whether through the Bible or his new faith, he had a peace and comfort he'd never known before. His attitude was so different his shipmates teased him about becoming a preacher.

Then one day the young man had a beautiful dream. He'd fallen asleep while en route to the Mediterranean. Since all the other work had been done, the crew was enjoying some free time. During this dream, God spoke to the young man and told him he was calling him to preach and to share what God had done for him. When he awoke, he went to find Curtis and tell him of the dream. Curtis was polite as ever, but pointed out the young man does have a speech problem and isn't very educated. Maybe he's just had a pleasant, fanciful dream. He is probably reading the Bible too much, fueling his imagination. God will understand if he takes a break from all that reading. When they return to port they'll go see the preacher. Butch can tell him the dream and see what he has to say about it. Butch agreed with Curtis's advice. After all, he's more mature in the things of God than Butch is. Curtis was raised in the church and Butch had only gone forward a little while ago. In fact, it'd be more likely God would choose Curtis over him. Yeah, Curtis is right. He is getting overly religious and letting his imagination run away with him. It was a silly idea to believe God would ever call someone like him.

~~Weekend liberty came ~~

They were at sea for a while. But finally, the day came when they were back in port. The weekend liberty finally came and they headed back to Ohio. Curtis said it's going to be great this weekend because the young people's group has a special outing. The pastor has agreed to listen to Butch's dream. The weekend went by nicely and Sunday evening was soon there. Butch shared his dream with the pastor with a heart filled with hope. The pastor called him over and said, "Young man, look at all of my young people. They are the cream of the crop. God can choose any one of them. Why would He want a freak like you? Young man, you're nothing but trouble, a street punk! You can't even speak right! And you think God wants you? What's wrong with you? I told Curtis the first time he brought you, he was wasting his time. Surely, there are others aboard the ship he can bring. But, he insists you are sincere. As far as I am concerned, you can leave the church and never come back! I don't care!"

"Sir, are you saying God doesn't want me? Are you saying you and your church don't want me? Is that right? What have I done? Why do you despise me so much?"

~~ Turning Back ~~

"Well, son, it's really not your fault. There are some people who just aren't meant to be saved. They're just born with a defective character. You happen to be one of them. Oh, you probably think you're saved and feel pretty good. But, that won't last long. You'll crave your old ways. Like the dog you'll go back to your vomit. You'll just go back to your old ways. You can't help it. You are simply predestined for damnation!"

Anger rose up in Butch. He wanted to violently strike this representative of the God of Christianity. If he did, he'd prove the old fool right. The young man was sincere that day at the altar. Sure, he didn't start on his own down the isle. But he finished on his own! What was it about him that even God couldn't forgive and love? Butch just shook his head and stated, "Well, if you and your God don't want me; then I don't want you. Keep your so-called church. Don't worry. I won't be back!"

He walked away as the Pastor watched.

29
HOMEWARD BOUND

He walked away from the pastor who had ripped out his heart. After this vicious assault, the pastor acted as if nothing was wrong. He watched the pastor put his arm around the shoulders of some of the young men and laughed with them. He watched as the pastor joked with some of the young girls and spoke to the parents. He saw their fellowship. But there was no fellowship for him! Curtis walked up to him and asked how it went. Butch told him what the pastor had said. Curtis said, "I don't think he means God doesn't want you in the church. He just doesn't want you in the ministry with him. Look how the pastor accepts Harris and David from the ship. Don't let this bother you. At least the pastor can set you straight before you end up in prison like that other dreamer Joseph!"

"Joseph?" Butch asked.

"You know." said Curtis, "That guy in the Bible who dreamed his father and brothers would bow down to him some day. His father tried to warn him to keep his dream to himself. But, he wouldn't. Look what happened to him! He was almost murdered by his brothers and ended up as a slave, and then in prison! Listen to the pastor and follow his advice. Or your life could end up like Joseph's. Come on, it's time to head back. Didn't I say you'd have a great time this weekend? And the pastor was able to do away with that fanciful dream. You'll probably never dream that dream again. You'll probably be able to get some sleep, now. Don't you feel better?" The two men arrived back at the ship. Curtis was still talking about the great weekend and how much the pastor must have helped with all his wisdom he had shared.

~~ The Return Home ~~

When the two were halfway down the pier and almost to the gangway leading to the quarter deck, some of the crew leaned over the rail and shouted, "Hey, Louis, look at the list in the mess hall! You're up six months early for discharge! The government is cutting back on its military size." Butch couldn't believe it! His name was on the list for early discharge. He had two days left to muster out. He was a civilian again! On the morning of his last day, he was leaving the bulk of the ship to the mid ship. He was met by a loud mouth petty officer that has been riding him for days about anything. Butch's mind was on the pastor's words. Was the pastor right? Was the young man destined to damnation, no matter what he did? The petty officer had picked a bad time to run his mouth. As he ascended the stairs shouting at Butch, the young man reminded him that in about two minutes he'd be a civilian. He didn't have to listen to him. Hassen made the biggest mistake in his life! He kept running his mouth. His head came up even with Butch's foot. Butch let go with all the anger built up within him with a kick that shattered Hassen's nose, and jaw, and left him out cold on the main deck of the ship. Butch walked over to the body of the unconscious petty officer and muttered, "Have a nice day."

He was finally out of the Navy and on his way to the bus station. On the way he remembered why he hated the city. All it meant to him was trouble. As he tried to buy his ticket home; one of the locals was telling everyone who'd listen to him, or wouldn't listen, how he hated the Navy. All sailors were punks. Just before the young man's fist struck the local's jaw, he bragged he never met a sailor he couldn't beat in a fight. As the lights went out, he realized he just met one! For the second

time, since the day began, Butch stepped over the body of a
loud mouth. On the Greyhound bus ride home from Virginia,
Butch had a lot to think about. One thing for sure, he wouldn't
let the words of that pastor influence him or rob him of his joy.
He'd truly met God in that little church and surely God had not
rejected him. When he arrived home, he'd find a church.
Maybe someday the pastor of the church in Ohio would see
him and realize how much he'd grown. Then he'd have to
apologize for his cruel and careless words. Butch still had his
Bible. He could read that. He hadn't found a church, though. In
fact, didn't Ola tell him Shiva wanted him to continue going to
church?

When he arrived home he found things hadn't really changed.
In fact if they had, it was only for the worse. The gang was
heavily into drugs and the projects were worse then ever. Both
of his sisters were on their own. Martin's apartment was
cluttered with old televisions and radios everywhere. Butch
applied for his 5250, which was his right to claim for one year
after his discharge. He'd collect $50.00 a week. After standing
in line for two weeks, he decided he'd better find work.

~~ Back to the old Job ~~

He went back to the same factory he worked at before he
enlisted in the navy. He worked for two weeks before he lost
his temper on the job. He stuck the foreman, head first, into the
trash container and walked off the job. Life sucked and he was
thinking of going back into the service. Then his circumstances
changed and he landed a decent job with the state as an
assistant cook. The job also provided living quarters on the
grounds and after 90 days he couldn't be fired! That was
helpful considering his bad temper. For a while everything was
going good .He managed to stay out of trouble on the job and
the staff seemed to like him. After work, Butch would go to the
projects to hang out with the guys and check in on his father.
Things were pretty quiet, except for the occasional gang fights
over turf rights. Everything was pretty mellow.

Then, two things happened which caused him to walk away from the projects forever. The first happened one night when the gang was partying. Two young boys ran up to the corner yelling. They'd found a couple of dead bodies. The gang went to investigate and found two young girls lying unconscious on the ground. One had a hypodermic needle still hanging from her vein. Butch told one of the young boys to go to the girl's parent's house and tell them to call for help. He worked on the two for a long time and was finally able to revive them. When the ambulance finally arrived they were able to sit up and gave good responses to questions asked. They were taken to the hospital. Later that night, the gang found out that the two girls had shot water into their veins to see if they could get high. It almost cost them their lives!

The second incident involved one of the two girls. It seemed she was dating a rival gang member. One day, when he was angry; he beat her just because she lived in the projects. Once the story got back to her brother, he demanded revenge for what was done to his sister. Before the gang counsel, he claimed it was his right to ask for the gang to go to war. Not only was his sister beaten, but also she was beaten because she was one of them! This made it a gang matter! Everyone voted for war. The acting warlord asked Butch if he'd lead the battle. He said he would. When the gang arrived at the other territory, they found only three members of the rival gang. After beating them, they left a message for their leaders. They let them know where they could be found.

~~ The Hidden Object ~~

The gang was back on their turf in the projects. After about three hours, four carloads of the rival gang showed up. The war was on! The battle was just about over when Butch caught the rival gang leader. The two began to fight. The other man suddenly swung around and hit Butch dead center in the stomach with a hard object. That object turned out to be a large hunting knife! As soon as Butch saw the knife sticking out of his stomach, he hit the man twice with a tire iron on the side of his head. The fighting stopped immediately. Everyone stared at Butch, expecting him to collapse. The other leader was already down on his knees. The knife was stuck, hard! Butch couldn't pull it out! He glanced at the other gang members, and then looked down with surprise to see there wasn't any blood! Someone was definitely looking out for him! The large knife was wedged firmly into his oversized belt buckle!

~~ Walked Away ~~

Standing there, he thought, "I almost died tonight for no reason at all! This gang honor is ridiculous and definitely not worth dying for." Turning around, he looked at Sammy who was the warlord and handed him the tire iron he'd used in the battle. "Sammy, it's all yours! You can have it. There's no purpose to our lives. As lousy as they are, I'm not going to waste mine over foolishness like this!" Butch turned and walked away. Thinking to himself, 'twice he was shot at with a shotgun. He'd been fired at with a pistol. Tonight was the second time someone had stabbed him." Each time, he was more than lucky. But, he knew his luck wouldn't last forever. If he had to die, it won't be for a foolish reason. When he returned to his room that night, he had a visitor waiting for him. Once again, Ola, spirit of the dead, confronted him. He wasn't surprised to see him. Of course it would be Ola who would take him to the land of the dead; to the kingdom of his father?

Ola spoke, "You were very fortunate tonight. If your father had not a purpose for you, it would've been your time! You'd be in the land of the dead! Not as a prince but as a failure! Your father doesn't treat failures lightly! Don't be stupid and place yourself in unnecessary danger. Let the fools fight! Let the fools fight their own battles! Let them lead themselves. A man who leads an army of fools is no better than those fools he leads! Always remember that!

Your father, the great Shiva, isn't pleased with you, at all! It's time you separated from your past, for your own good. Start training seriously once again to rule with your father! Is that clear to you, boy?"

"Yes, Ola. Tell my father that I, also, am not pleased with myself, tonight. My days with the gang are over. I will apply myself to study."

After Ola left, Butch began to look at his life. He had a good job. He had his own place to live. He had friends outside of the projects. But, he wasn't really happy. Perhaps if he studied harder, he would truly find peace.

~~ Something still missing ~~

Tonight was the first time, since he left the Navy; he'd spoken to any of his guides. Maybe, he needed to return to daily communication with them. In fact, none of the elders had been around him for a long time. All communication had come to a complete halt. He knew they were around because he could feel them watching him. But, they wouldn't approach him. It seemed as if even his father, the master, was afar off and avoiding him. He sent Ola to speak to him, but didn't come himself. Was he angry? Had he offended Shiva through his foolishness? All of a sudden he felt strongly compelled to grab the Bible Curtis' mother had given him. Picking up the book, he opened it to Genesis and the life of Abraham. He was impressed. Every time Abraham wanted to talk to God he would build an altar and pray to him. That was it! Tomorrow he'd find a secret place and build an altar to the God of the universe and he would speak to Him. Just maybe this would please his father and he would visit and explain what was going on. The powers were increasing and getting stronger every day. But, he wasn't able to control them any longer. It was as if they were too powerful for him. On the job he could hear what people around him were thinking. He could read their minds as easily as he could read a book. The power to move things with his mind was also growing. He couldn't always control it. That was what the mentors were for. They were supposed to be showing him how to control the power. For now, it seemed the powers controlled him! He truly needed to talk to Shiva; especially after tonight! But, just because he needed to talk, didn't mean Shiva would reply.

∼ The altar ∼

Butchs' mind was confused. He needed answers! The next day, right after work, Butch began searching for answers. He felt strongly compelled to pick-up the Bible that Curtis' mother had given him. Picking up the book, he opened it to the life of Abraham. Reading he was impressed that every time Abraham wanted to talk to God he would build an altar, and pray to him. *That was it! That's the answer. Build an altar. Tomorrow he would find a secret place, and build an altar to the God of the universe,* and he would speak to Him. Just maybe this would please his father, and he would visit, and explain what was going on. The next day he went to the woods and found the perfect place for an altar. He gathered stones as Abraham did and laid them on top of each other. There he knelt every day and prayed calling on the God of the universe to hear him and to speak with him. Yet, Shiva, his so-called father would not reply.

Two weeks passed. One day, while hanging around with some of the student nurses and other workers, they got into a discussion about religion and God. He told them he wasn't of his mother's religion. He didn't believe in their teachings. The church in Ohio showed him they are deceived in these lies and falsehoods. "Well, what is the difference between what that church believes and what his mom believed?" one of the nurses asked.

He didn't really know too much about the church in Ohio or what they believed. But he answered, honestly. All he knew was they didn't pray to the saints or to Mary. Also, they didn't believe in confessing their sins to a man; only to God! Oh, yeah, one other thing. Jesus wasn't nailed to their cross any-more! They said he wasn't there 'cause He is alive! *He is risen!*

"We know He's risen!" one of the girls responded, "but our church teaches; when the priest recites the Mass, He's once again crucified for our sins. That's why He's so angry with us! So we have to go to Mary so she can intercede on our behalf."

"Well, that's where their church differs from yours, too. They say only Jesus is our mediator and no one can go to the Father except through Jesus! No one is equal to Jesus and everyone is born with sin and gone astray! But, the Ohio church says the Bible claims all have sinned and come short of the glory of God! We need to accept Jesus as Lord and Savior!"

"Well," replied the girl, "I don't know about all that. All I know is I was born a Catholic and I will die one. I agree with the church. There's no salvation outside of the Roman Catholic Church!"

"Man," said his friend, "let's get off this religious talk. *All roads lead to Rome.* You know, there's more than one way to God; if He does exist. As far as I'm concerned; there is no God, heaven or hell! If there is, He's too busy to care about us. Come on! Let's go to the beach and have some fun."

"You guys go," said Butch. "I'm going to stay and workout some questions I have. I'll see you later."

30
THE ANSWER COMES

When everyone left, Butch went back to his secret place. *It was an altar that he had built in the woods.* **He intended to stay there until he received his answer.** He sat down on an old tree stump. He was deep in meditation when he heard a voice say, "Hello!" When he opened his eyes, a young woman he'd never seen before, was standing before him. "Who are you and what do you want?"

"My name is Shannon and it's not about what I want. It's about what you want and have been asking god for."

"What do you mean?" Butch asked.

Shannon asked, **"Have you not been praying to God? Asking him to show himself to you? Haven't you been building an altar to him?'**

"How do you know this?" asked Butch

Shannon replied, **"I know this because *God* has sent me to you. *Butch never questioned what God.*** I know about the increase of your powers and your inability to control them. I know you feel your father is far from you, and he's turned his back on you. In spite of what you feel, this is not true! He sent

175

me to train you and to teach you how to control your powers. He also sent me to show you the truth about religion, so you won't be confused. He allowed you to go to that church in Ohio, so you could see how false they are. Look how those hypocrites preach love and then judge and condemn everyone else. They arrogantly believe no one but their little group is saved! My, how boring heaven would be if they controlled it. Look what the pastor did to you! Was that love when he told you God didn't need a punk like you? You couldn't even speak right? Oh, these so called Christian's preach a good game, but their lives betray the lies they preach! The Bible you've been reading is a good book. But remember, imperfect men wrote it! So, what makes it anymore holy than the Koran, I Ching or the Book of Shadows? They're all religious, written by dedicated believers of their faiths. How can you put one above the other? Don't you understand god is in all things? God is in you and you are in god! In fact, you are a god! Doesn't the God of the Bible say we're all gods and there were many gods? That's why I'm here to help you reach your god-consciousness and to release the god-self who is trapped within you; because of your flesh. Remember, knowledge is power! Without it, no soul can evolve to a higher plain." Shannon and Butch talked for hours. She showed him new meditation exercises, which helped him to control his powers. He was very impressed with her knowledge of religion and the Bible. *She showed him how to use the Bible and even the name of Jesus to work magic!* They began to work with others and to increase the size of their own following. They were very particular concerning whom they invited in. Only serious minded students were accepted. The circle increased. They began to meet twice a month, then weekly.

Butch was given his *athame, sword, cup, and cap.* One day, Shannon gave him a blank book. She told him it was his own Book of Shadows. He was to write his personal spells in it. After about three months, Shannon gave him *a necklace and a bracelet consisting of* blue, black, purple and red beads. There was one thing that stood out on his bracelet, which wasn't on any of the other items. *It was a symbol of a double red cross!*

176

"This," Shannon said, *"was a symbol of his position and authority.* Wherever he went, every one of the societies would recognize him for who he was."

Shannon had finished her routines at the institution and was back at her school in Springfield. The two of them kept in touch by telepathy. They could communicate from distances of over a hundred and twenty miles. They reached a point where they could move objects with their minds and astral-project their spirits at will. ***Whatever they commanded and proclaimed came to pass. There was no limitation!***

~~The uninvited visitors ~~

One night when Butch was alone in his room, three beings appeared without being invited or summoned! Except for Ola and Chango, his spirit guides, this had never happened before!

When he challenged their authority and right to be there he received no answer. Using a protective spell, he took authority over them and commanded them to leave. The three turned and walked through the wall facing the street and vanished! When Butch looked out the window to the ground three floors below; they were nowhere in sight. He began to feel uncomfortable with what he'd just seen. He immediately called forth Ola and Chango and asked what was going on. Did they know who these spirits were? Chango spoke up and said they are three evil spirits sent by other witches to try to destroy him and take his powers. He must not worry, for Chango and Ola will take care of these spirits for their trespass.

Then Chango looked at him and told him it was time for him to take his convent name. Write it in his blood; in his Book of Shadows. He must be careful, though. There is a traitor who is close to him who will try to take his position and powers. Butch must not trust anyone; not even his closest friend! Chango revealed that in the month of October, at a chosen time and place, the master would arrange for a secret meeting. He will summon the top occult leaders. Butch will be appointed as the head of all positions of leadership! *He will receive this anointing at the hands of his father and master, Lord Shiva!*

Butch couldn't believe the day was finally coming when his master would recognize him. And in front of all of his major followers! It's a dream come true! With one more word of warning about the traitor, Chango and Ola vanished! Who could this traitor be? Chango said it was someone close to him. But his best friend isn't a believer. He doesn't believe in anything but money. Well, he'll just call Shannon and get together. They can cast a revealing spell and find out who the traitor is.

The next two weeks were so busy, with meetings; he had no chance to get together with Shannon to cast that spell. Two incidents caused Butch to take a step back and look at those around him. Both involved Shannon. One was personal and the other business. Shannon revealed her feelings for him. She expressed her interested in more than just a business a relationship with him. Butch told her it would never be. He didn't consider her anything more than a mentor and friend.

The second incident was business. Shannon brought a group of witches who wanted to join with them and form a union together. They desired to control the New England states. Butch found out this group weren't witches, but Satanists! He refused to have anything to do with them. A serious argument, with Shannon, came about over the doctrine of Satanism verses witchcraft. Eventually she agreed not to fellowship with them.

About two weeks after the second incident, Shannon got in touch with him. She requested a meeting as soon as possible! The two met at Shannon's apartment. The young man asked what problem was so serious that a meeting had to be set. She told him she felt the group was loosing power and prestige. Some important problems had to be worked out, quickly! The

coven needed to know which direction they were to go in.
Butch interrupted her and said he needed to use the restroom.
Shannon smiled and said, "Good, perhaps when you come back
things will be clear. You'll see who the hindrance is. Then
you'll know what must be done to solve this problem."

~~ The truth is revealed ~~

When he entered the restroom, the first thing he saw was a
large picture of *Baphometh,* the goat; with a shrine directly
under it! "What is that picture doing in your bathroom? You
know what that represents! We don't agree with their
philosophy!"

"That's where you're so wrong!" Shannon yelled. "Maybe, you
aren't smart enough to know where your powers come from.
But I do! You're so blind and foolish! Wake up, **Butch! Open
your eyes, and see the truth for once! Your powers come
from Satan. He alone is your god. And the only god!"**

"You lie!" shouted Butch. ***"My father is Shiva! He's not a
devil!*** We receive our powers from him! Now, I understand.
And yes, Shannon, I will open my eyes and look upon my
Judas! You are the one who seeks to betray me! Do you truly
believe, oh foolish witch, you can beat me? Take my powers?
Do you really believe you can truly destroy me and rule in my
place in my father's kingdom?" Anger flashed in his eyes.
Before Shannon could do anything to protect herself, **Butch
released an energy fire blast!** It not only destroyed her
power and left her defenseless. It nearly took her life!

~~ A Warning ~~

Standing over her prone, nearly lifeless body, he strongly
warned her. "Shannon, as long as you're involved in this
garbage, don't ever cross my path, again! If you do, not only
will I take what power you have left; I will take your life!
Chango and Ola warned me about a traitor. They told me not to

trust anyone. They were so right! I made a terrible mistake! I let you into my life. I trusted you as a friend and mentor. I promise I will never make that mistake again! Watch what you do and say. If I even hear a whisper you're planning anything, I'll be back!"

31
THE POWER - THE UNHOLY ANOINTING

Butch walked into the bathroom and took the picture down. He threw it in the trash. He turned and walked out of the apartment. He'd never set foot in there, again! Yet, that apartment would affect his life until the day he died. *The powerful month of October* was soon upon him. One night, while he was meditating, his room was suddenly filled with raw power! He dropped to his knees immediately and lowered his head. In the center of the room stood Shiva, the Destroyer; in his entire splendor! Shiva spoke! *"On the fourth of October* you are to go to West Port; to the beach. There you will strip yourself of all your clothing and meditate until I appear to you. When I do, I will call the counsel of my choice to watch your ordination. In the midst of the people I shall proclaim you, my son, as their king! Now, make yourself ready for the day is almost here. ***Have you chosen your name? Your new name is very important for the kingdom***."

~~ The name change ~~

"Yes, master." replied Butch. "I've chosen the name **Marcus Judas**" For some strange reason the name Judas came to mind."

"It is good!" Shiva proclaimed. *"From this day forth, you shall be known in my kingdom as Marcus Judas, King of Witches; Son of Shiva*. No one may bear that name, forever. There will only be one Marcus Judas; for all time! So say I, Shiva, lord of all!" Before Butch could respond, Shiva vanished and the room returned to normal. The name Marcus didn't bother him. He'd personally chosen that name after Marc Anthony. But the name Judas troubled him. He hadn't chosen that name. It was as if someone placed that name in his mind and branded it upon his heart! The only Judas he knew was the one in the Bible who betrayed Jesus. Why would he want that name? He hadn't betrayed Christ? In fact, he'd tried to be a follower of Jesus? But, the church wouldn't let him! The pastor said he wasn't good enough. So he simply came back where he belonged. Why did that name bother him? He was no traitor. Oh, well, Shiva was pleased with the name. From this day forth, he'd be known, forever, in the kingdom of Shiva as Marcus Judas, son of Shiva, King of Witches!

∼ The ceremony begins ∼

October fourth was only two days away. There was much for him to prepare. October fourth came. It was the coldest day he could remember in a long time. It was record setting cold! Well below freezing. But, Butch did as he was told. He was at the beach at sunset as instructed. He stripped off all his clothes, except for his briefs and sat in the lotus position. A dozen elders surrounded him in a semi-circle. Shiva, himself, summoned all! He personally selected these proven warriors who had earned the right and honor to observe and bear witness to the ceremony, which was performed that night!

After three hours of below zero weather an apparition appears! At first rising, slowly out of the water. Expecting to see Shiva, the group is surprised to see the appearance of the three-faced goddess of the Wicca's known as Hecarte! Hecarte slowly approaches the group. Now, frozen not only because of the weather, but also because of her appearance; they are totally blown away!

Shiva suddenly appears by her right side; the side of power! The two deities joined arms and slowly, regally walked to the young man who has been seated on the beach, in the lotus position, for over three hours, in this record setting freeze! Hectare immediately lays her hands on Butch! She begins to speak in an *unknown tongue.*

Then, **both beings lay hands on his head and Shiva begins to pray in an unknown language.** When he finishes the prayer, he raises both his head and his hands. He loudly proclaims to all gathered there, *"Behold, my beloved son! In whom I am well pleased. Do to him what you would do to me! What you give him, you are giving to me! What you hold back from him, you hold back from me! Bless him, and you bless me! Strike him and you strike me! Behold, Marcus Judas, son of Shiva, King of Witches, so say I, Shiva, the Destroyer, lord of ALL!"*

Hecarte, who'd been standing quietly as Shiva spoke, now lifted her faces and spoke. "So must it be even as it has been spoken, let it come to pass! All ye are gathered here listen to what Shiva has said! And take heed, also, to what I say in agreement. Marcus Judas, son of Shiva, King of Witches, blessed be your name among witches forever! Let no one dare bear that name except for thee, Oh, Great Son of Shiva!" *Butch could feel overwhelming power flowing from the hands of Shiva; penetrating from the top of his head, throughout his whole body.* It dawned on him; not only was Shiva **transferring power to him; he was transferring authority and the nature of Shiva's own spirit in order to be as one.** Shiva once again spoke to the counsel, "Let the celebration begin!"

The party began. Everyone was celebrating. Butch tried to stand from his lotus position. As he got to his feet, he lost his balance. He reached out to one of the women next to him dressed in a fur coat. As he grabbed her arm to brace him, the woman began to scream! The heat from his hand burned through the coat and severely burnt her arm! Shiva approached the woman and touched her arm. The pain left instantly but the coat was still burnt! Shiva looked at Butch. He said this was *proof of the anointing* Butch just received. He was now ordained to be a powerful ruler. Shiva also told him, if need be, he could call forth fire to destroy his enemy! But he must be careful with the use of his powers! Shiva observed the party as the group danced, sang, and worshiped him. He walked among them. Hecarte, the goddess of the witches encouraged Butch as they praised Shiva.

~~ The Kingdom taken back ~~

Shiva told the celebrants to be patient a little longer. For his son had come into his inheritance. **His kingdom will be established!** The world will be his! Once and for all! **Those who were faithful and submit to him will rule with him**. The followers of the so-called Jewish Messiah will be their slaves forever. Their beloved Messiah will be tortured forever! Everyone cheers and shouts as the mighty Destroyer, Shiva and his escort Hecarte, raise their hands one last time to bless the group. Shiva suddenly vanishes from sight! The celebration came to an end shortly after Hecarte left. Everyone went his or her separate ways. Butch could sense division. Not all were happy. Not all were in agreement with their master's words. For now, they'll follow. Some out of love and dedication, but mostly they'll follow out of fear! They'll abide their time. They'll patiently wait for their chance to usurp Butch's authority and take his position. For now, though, he is their earthly ruler and must be obeyed. Shiva has spoken! To disobey means your life! There are no second chances!

It is Butchs' responsibility to unite the different groups of witches. He must gather together a league. They must set aside their differences for the sake of the craft! To form a league and bring unity among the Wiccans will be hard enough; never mind including witches and Satanists! These groups have never been willing to set aside their authority and power to submit to another. In fact, most of these people would never obey or submit to a so-called king. To come under a king means there is only one way to the God and Goddesses. This is contrary to the belief of all cultists! They all believed there are many ways to utopia. There is no need for a king! Why should they, who've been in power for so long, submit to a young upstart; just because the master proclaims him as his son? It doesn't mean they must to submit to even the master's will! Although, the master is powerful, and a god; he is not the only god! Doesn't their religion teach there are many gods? All they need to do is submit to a god, stronger than Shiva. In fact, doesn't the Hindu's legend teach that Kali, the many-armed goddess of the Hindu's, known as the wife of Shiva, the Destroyer, can actually control Shiva? In many ways she is his equal! If they will serve her faithfully, won't she protect them against Shiva? They'll go along with the command of Shiva, for a while. But when it becomes to be too much, they'll rebel. Don't the gods need them just as much as they need the Gods?

The first attack came sooner then anyone had expected. It came from a self-proclaimed king of Satanists! He refused to submit to a new comer who didn't even have enough sense to know Satan was his Lord. All occultists worship Satan! Knowingly or unknowingly! No matter what name they called their god or goddess, all religion leads to the same god! Since the Satanist was the first to build a church in America to the great dark lord; he'd be damned if he'd bow to a mere man! No matter what title he was supposed to have. He'd simply destroy this young punk. Take whatever feeble powers he had and make him his eternal slave. He could always use a footstool for his throne in hell. He will rule with Satan, his great dark lord! What better footstool could there be then this so-called son of Shiva! *The actual attack* lasted only a few hours. But, as his son testified, the Satanist spent the rest of his life hating and cursing the son of Shiva. The only man he could never defeat!

After this battle, witches across the country, although they would not submit to him, were afraid and vowed not to attack him. After the defeat of the Satanist, no one openly dared attack. Everyone knew of the Satanists great powers!

The second attack came from nearer to home. A former solitary practitioner who felt, by defeating Butch, he'd not only take the young man's coven from him, but his powers and authority as well! He knew he'd be a much stronger leader with his modern outlook on life and his powerful blend of Wicca and new age philosophy. He would lead the faithful out of the mental dungeons of the Dark Age and the old traditional ways of the so-called son of Shiva. Ronny might reluctantly admit Butch could be the son of Shiva, a minor God. But Ronny's religious philosophy convinced him he was a god in the embryo stage! One day, through true spiritual evolution, he'll become a mighty god! He'll rule his own universe! Shiva will always be what he always was; a lower demi-god, ruling parts of this mud hole called earth. But Ronny the great, will rule universes! First, he'll have to destroy this upstart, wanna be King of Witches! Of course, when he does, all of the other witches of all the different schools will be so grateful they'll willingly submit to him! For is he not their great liberator? Setting all witches free from the rule of this self imposed dictator? Ronny doubted the story of the impartation from both Shiva and Hecarte. He didn't believe the proclamation supposedly made by Shiva. He didn't believe that Butch was *Shiva's* son and his appointed king. Even if this were true, *not even Shiva, the so-called* **Destroyer** could stand in the way of Ronny, the magnificent, the greatest of all avastars ever to exist! Not even Mohammad or Jesus had reached his level of enlightenment! So, how could Shiva stand a chance against someone so totally in tune and at one with Brahma, the cosmo-consciousness? Ronny pitied poor *Shiva* if he tried to intervene and stop the overthrow of his so-called son. It was a good thing Ronny was so compassionate. He wouldn't destroy Butch, completely. He'd simply drain him of his powers He'd retrain this pretender and reform him into Ronny's image! Ronny's plan was awesome and flawless! It was just too bad he never got the chance to implement it. Before he even began, he was completely destroyed! The next time Ronny was seen in public, the self-proclaimed greatest *avastar* to ever grace the planet, was found sitting in a lotus position, glibly conversing with a rock! It'll be a long time before he comes back to his senses. When he finally did, he was no longer an avastar. He's now a faithful member of a local Kingdom Hall!

The final attack directed at Butch once more proved, the words of Chango and Ola, to be true. No one could be trusted! Not even his closest friend! The attack came in the middle of the night as Butch lay sleeping. Suddenly! Out of nowhere, three powerful witches appeared in his room! He barely had time to awaken and summon a spell of protection before the attack began! At the end of the battle, minutes later, the three witches were banished and stripped of their powers! The name of the leader was given over. She turned out to be one of his loyal coven members. He personally brought this one up through the three levels of initiation that were required for those desiring leadership positions in the coven. Butch was just days away from setting her over her own coven! He was going to establish her as the high priestess of the area. She was to rule by his side. She would be under no one but him! Yet this was not enough for Elaina!

~~ I am woman   Hear me roar ~~

She wasn't satisfied with this. She wanted it all! Wasn't this the 70's? This is the Time of Enlightenment and the dawn of the Age of Aquarius! Due to the *spirit of the feminist* movement, women were coming into power as a separate identity; away from the man and patriarchal authority. Their voice was being heard everywhere. They were coming out from under the shadow of men. They were coming into their rightful position of power!

~~ Wasn't witchcraft a feminist religion? ~~

Wasn't the woman more powerful than the male? Why should she submit to a man? No matter who he was! She is female! She is at one with the goddess! She is meant to rule over all! All men are to be her slaves! Once she destroyed the son of Shiva, the so-called King of Witches, then the coven will line up properly. Just like a beehive or an anthill, where the queen rules unopposed! All others were merely workers; existing only to please the queen. When his newest opponent was exposed, Butch resorted to ritual magic! He waited for the proper time and position of the moon.

~~ The spell of Retribution ~~

Drawing the required symbols and using the suggested candles and charms; he called for the Law of Retribution to be put into effect. This law calls for the innocent to be avenged! Everything had to be perfect or the spell would return more powerful than when it was cast! Very few ever survived the backlash of this spell. If they did, they were left as an emotional cripple, for life! Their families were completely destroyed! The power of this spell, when it was released, knocked out the power over two square miles. *Elaina, the would be Queen of Witches! Elaina, who would dominate and rule all men!* Elaina no longer knew her name! She would end up spending years in institutions for the mentally impaired. The struggle for leadership was finally over. No body dared come forth to challenge him. It seemed, at last, he'd be able to bring to pass the will of Shiva. Finally, the plan of the master would be fulfilled! Shiva's incarnation will be completed through his son, Marcus Judas, King of Witches! His kingdom will be established. Its proper Lord will finally rule the earth! Heaven will tremble and hell will rejoice! The master will finally be avenged! Butch had a successful meeting with his old guides. It was actually an enjoyable time. He hadn't spent much time with either of the two for quite a while. It seemed, the further he went up the ladder of authority, the less he saw of his guides. Now is a time of celebration!

∼ The Indwelling ∼

The great night of the indwelling was rapidly coming. On this chosen night, Shiva will actually become one with his son, Marcus Judas, by indwelling and possessing him completely! On this night of nights, the master known as Shiva, the Destroyer, will fulfill the Hindu legend. The night tiger, which walks like a man, will manifest! This will be accomplished by Shiva completely possessing the spirit and soul of Butch. He will no longer be a mere mortal but a god manifested in the flesh!

The dream of his mother, so many years ago, giving birth to a son who would become god and savior of his people was about to come to pass! She would be so proud!

But the enemy's Book calls those who are so completely possessed by another spirit, beasts. All will agree there has never been a beast such as this!

32
IT IS FINISHED!

After his guides left, Butch sat alone in his room. His mind dwelt on his mother. He wished she'd lived to see her dreams fulfilled. To see this reality! He pictured her filled with joy, smiling as she realized all of the promises were finally coming to pass! In spite of everything that came against him, he managed to go from a crippled nobody to the incarnation of the mighty Shiva! When his **kingdom is finally established**, he'll place his mother at his side. Then she'll receive the respect she so rightly deserved. After all, if he is king, shouldn't his mother be queen? Wouldn't this be an incredible opportunity for the great Shiva to show forth his resurrection power and raise her from the dead? Was he not the Lord of all creation? Now that his kingdom was going to be established forever on this earth; surely, this will be a small thing for him to do for his son! Butch sat in total amazement. Finally, in one more day, it'll be over. Things will be as they should have been from the beginning of time!

~~ Time to reflect ~~

He ran through the thoughts in mind. He began to think about his recent victories in battle. He realized no one could stand against him! His was the ultimate power that so many had sought for so long. Who could stand against him? Who could defeat him? He was unconquerable! His was the ultimate victory. His mind was filled with arrogance and his heart with pride. Nobody but Shiva was his equal! Who'd dare be so foolish as to ever try to challenge him again? He wasn't just a man, but a god! He thought about this, deeply, as he laid his head down to sleep. He was on top of the world. He was rightfully a King of the Witches; the spiritual son of Shiva, the magnificent. His kingdom would be established forever. His life was only going to get better and better!

~~ The Lie ~~

Within a few minutes he was sound asleep. Suddenly! Like a snare, in less then a microsecond his world was changed forever and ever! Everything he studied and grew to believe as the truth was eternally altered! It was not inspirational truth! It was a lie straight from the infernal of hell! It was created to deceive as many as possible by the father of lies! Lucifer! Known as the prince of darkness, the great archangel overcome and thrown out of heaven by Michael, the archangel; by God's authority! The fantasy of his life of lies was shattered forever. In a split moment of time, all hope was gone forever! He'll never know the splendor of ruling his own kingdom with his mother by his side. He could only see the horror! He only saw eternal damnation and separation from the only true God of creation! Butch had just entered his room moments before. He lay down and closed his eyes and fell into a deep sleep.

~~ Welcome to Hell ~~

Suddenly, his spiritual eyes were opened as never before! Welcome to Hell! This is the prison for rebellious spirits! This is the place of intense darkness and total isolation. The eyes can't see anything! Not even his own hand held right in front of his face! There was no doubt in his mind. He knew exactly where he was! How could this have happened to him? Was he not the king of witches, the only begotten son of powerful Shiva? Did not his father rule all things? How could this be? How could he, of all people, end up in this place of eternal torment? Everything within cried out, "Why am I here?" It was a strange question. He already truly knew the answer! He profoundly knew he justly deserved to be here, and worse! Yet, it was as if mercy was being extended to him one last time. When at first he screamed out his question, he didn't really expect an answer to come. But even in this most dreadful of places he sensed a great compassion and grace!

~~ Out of the Great Darkness ~~

Out of the dread darkness a voice full of authority and immeasurable power greater than he had ever known or felt in his life, responded. ***"You are here because you serve you father, the devil! Unless you repent and call upon the name of My Son; you will spend eternity here!"***

"Who is your Son?" Butch cried out!

"He is Jesus!" thundered the voice, "and He alone is the only true Savior of mankind! No man can come unto Me unless they come through Him!"

"I am truly sorry!" cried Butch. "I believed you rejected me. That pastor even told me you had no need of me! He said I was a punk who couldn't even speak right. So why would you ever want me?"

"I did not tell you that. Did I?" questioned the voice. "If you had faith in Me and believed My Word instead of mans;' you'd have known I love you so much that I sent My own Son to take your place on the cross! I placed many people in your path to lead you to the truth! But you chose to believe and place your faith in a lie! You let the words of the foolish direct you away from a saving relationship with Me. You came so close to the truth, but you ran right back to your so-called father. Never once, did he show you love or mercy. But, no matter what he did to you or allowed to happen; you still blindly followed him! Know this! The road he led you on leads only to this place of torment in the end. This terrible place was never meant for man! It was made for the devil and his rebellious angels. But, because of each man's willful rebellion against me, I will place each rebellious man here! I have, in my great love and mercy, offered opportunity through My love, grace and Son's shed blood, to all men. I have done all to afford each man the opportunities to keep him from choosing this horrible end. I have paid for all their sins, in full, with my Son's blood! They are left with only one choice! Yet man, ignorant and arrogant, insists My ways are wrong and his is right! This is nothing but pride! The doors of salvation are open wide to anyone who desires it. Yes, it is a narrow road, which that leads to salvation. And it is only through Jesus that it can be found. But salvation is available to all who truly, simply accept it! Now, you are without excuse! The choice is yours. Turn from your evil ways. Renounce the God of this world, the prince of darkness.   Accept My free gift through My Son and His sacrifice for you as your personal Lord and Savior! Or continue in your foolish, arrogant, prideful spirit and spend all of eternity separated from me! *What say thee, Oh, King of Witches, thou mighty son of Shiva?"*

~~ My Yielding ~~

Butch humbly bowed his head and heart and confessed with his lips saying, "I yield to thee, Oh, Most High God and to Your Son, Jesus. I freely admit my pride. I am a sinner! I cannot save my self! I acknowledge that I alone am responsible for being in this place. Yet, I know I cannot stand against Shiva and his allies. I am doomed no matter what choice I make. I throw myself on your mercy and kindness great God. Two attributes I was always told were weak and feeble! If I am to die, it will be on Your side! Yet, I must sincerely ask one question. How can I ever make up for what I have already done against Your Kingdom, and for all those I have led astray?"

194

The voice replied, "Remember, My Salvation is by grace and grace alone! You can never repay what I have given you! No man can ever earn My free gift! I have given you a new heart of flesh and placed My Holy Spirit within your new heart; as a seal and a guarantee of the riches I have prepared for you in Christ Jesus! This is not by works! So no man may ever boast of his own merits. You can never make-up for what you have done. You can never buy my gifts! Neither can you earn forgiveness. It is a gift, freely given to all who earnestly forgive and sincerely ask for forgiveness from me. You have much to learn and a long way to go. Hold my hand and I will lead you. I have great plans for you! I will never leave you or forsake you!"

Butch asked, "How can I escape the wrath of Shiva? You may be a merciful, forgiving God; but he has never been merciful or forgiving! There is no way I can stand against him or defeat him in battle. I have seen what happens to those who try. The power of Shiva is unequaled by any being, anywhere! When Shiva speaks the earth shakes. At his commands sickness comes and death obeys! Ola and Chango, the Lord of Thunder and the Great Spirit of the Dead, are his faithful followers. They do his bidding. When he is angry, his vast army trembles in fear! How can I stand against one like him? Please, don't misunderstand me. I truly appreciate your generous offer and eagerly accept it! Yet my doom is sealed by accepting you as my Lord and Savior!"

"Who has told you this?" the voice demanded!

"It has been taught to me, over the years; by my guides. All the elders tell how Shiva was tricked, by You! He was tricked into giving up his position in heaven. They told me the faithful gave up their position to follow him, as he willingly left heaven, for a season. He also came to earth to influence mankind and to lead them out of darkness He came to teach them. To show them they were more than just animals, at the mercy of an uncaring God. They were actually gods themselves! They were trapped in this body of flesh. But

195

through the knowledge of good and evil, they could start their spiritual evolution to become just like You! Ola said all of Shiva's acts of kindness toward man angered You. Out of jealousy You proclaimed him a devil and banned him from heaven! Ola said You did this out of fear! You know when man is finally enlightened to their godhood, You will be overthrown! Then Shiva will be chosen to take Your place!"

The great voice gently replied saying, "That is quite the story; but nowhere near the truth! Man was made in My image and given the spirit, which I personally breathed into him. Man is not and will never be a God. Yet, he will be given the honor to rule and reign with my Son, the true King of Kings. Shiva was never a God or my equal. He is a creation. I, the Creator, by the power of My Holy Spirit, through My Son, Jesus Christ created him just as We created all the other angels! His own beauty blinded him. He was filled with pride. He tried to exalt his throne above mine! He was brought low, along with one third of the angels whom he deceived. He was cast out of heaven; by the hand of Michael, My archangel. Since then he's had a deep hatred of man! For not only is man created in My image, but Satan knows how much I care about each and every one of them. He knows he hurts me through the pain he causes them! Satan, in his bitterness, wrath and anger toward me has done all he can to, harm them, destroy them and lead them into damnation. Yes, Shiva is powerful; but he's a limited creation. Limited by Me! He is not all-powerful. Those who believe in Me, and in My Son, have absolute power over him and the works of all his allies! He is defeated by the blood of the Lamb. **He cannot stand against the Name of his God, My Son. Jesus!**

Jesus completely defeated him over two thousand years ago, on the cross. When My purpose for him is complete; I will one day surely bind him and cast him into the Lake of Fire! If you will listen to Me and do as I say, no weapon formed against you will prosper. You must destroy all of your materials on the occult and completely denounce all association with it. Walk away forever! When Shiva comes, you must call on the Name of My Son. You must also, daily, continually read My Word and hide it in your heart. Wash your soul in my Word, daily, as you wash your body. You will find it effective when you stand against his attacks. It will not be easy, but with My Spirit, you can do it and win! **He will lie to you and try to deceive you in order to keep you from your destiny and all I have planned for you in this life.** If you will remain humble, stand firmly in My Word and resist him, he will flee always from you! You will be Victorious! Now, go, and remember I will be with you always and forever!" Before Butch knew what happened, he was back in his room! His heart was racing! Yet he had a great peace. He was at peace with God for the first time in his life! He immediately gathered all of his occult books and materials. He packed them up. He put them in the basement of his sister's house until he could properly get rid of them. It would actually be over four years before he could destroy them!

33
THERE IS FREEDOM!
- FREEDOM REIGNS IN ME!

For a few days, nothing unusual occurred. Then, one night, while returning to his room, Butch was confronted by Ola and Chango, his former guides. They no longer pretended to be his friends. They immediately threaten him! Ola, spirit of the dead, began to laugh, as he revealed he was free to now do what he always wanted to do. Butch was no longer under the protection of the great Shiva! Shiva, himself, wanted Butch dead! Ola was given the pleasure of the assignment. Ola told Butch he was never worthy to be Shiva's son. Ola said he knew Butch never had what it takes to rule by Shiva's side. He told him he was weak. Once again, Ola told him he was there when Shiva had placed meningitis on him; when he was a baby. He was there when his mother made the deal; exchanging her life for his. Shiva enjoyed a great laugh with him over the whole situation.

Finally Chango interrupted. "Ola!" he snapped, "you talk too much! You're like these foolish human clay pots. You can't control your tongue. You're always running off at the mouth. We are ordered to destroy him. Do you think Shiva intends for you to talk him to death?" Ola's face flushed with extreme anger! His hands swiftly grasped his sword!

"Don't be foolish, Ola!" Chango said, menacingly. "If you draw your sword against me; the angel of the dead will experience death! Now, waste no more time! Let's quickly accomplish what we're required to do. Destroy this foolish mortal, now!" Butch was frozen on the spot. For the first time he truly knew dread fear! When Ola challenged him before, Shiva had protected Butch. Ola had to retreat. But now, Butch was no longer protected by the power of Shiva. His doom was unavoidable. There was no way out! Fear continued to dominate his heart and consume his numbing mind. There were no spells he could cast and no charms to protect him! No shield to defend him! If he has to die, he'll die as a man! He'll never allow these two to see fear in him. The God of creation promise him salvation! He may suffer in the body, but his spirit will go back to God! Just as Ola drew his sword and advanced toward him, an authoritative voice thundered from behind Butch! Ola shuddered for a moment!

The voice warned, "Touch not this one! He is claimed for the Most High, Lord God of Israel! Flinch! And you will be destroyed!" Ola and Chango froze where they stood and their terrible façade of confidence drained from their faces. Butch turned to see his defender. Standing directly behind him was the largest being he'd ever seen! Standing clearly over ten feet high! He was dressed in the most powerful of armor. His mighty sword looked as if it could cut a redwood tree in half with one stroke!

"My name is Michael!" said the giant. "I am here on behalf of the Lord God Almighty. He has claimed you and redeemed you because of the sacrifice of his Son, whom you have accepted by faith."

"You lackey of the Most High!' shouted Ola. "Do you think you can stand against the mighty spirit of the dead? With one blow of my sword it will be over for you foolish one! Now stand out of my way while I destroy this traitor to our great lord Shiva!"

Ola leaped forward and with the speed of light drew his sword! Yet, he was far too slow for the giant known as Michael. Faster then the blink of an eye, Michael drew his own immense weapon, and severed Ola in half and returned it to his hilt before Ola knew he was struck! The spirit of the dead joined his captured companions in that dark abyss; their great prison house of lost souls, awaiting their sure Day of Judgment. Michael immediately turned and faced Chango, the lord of thunder and lightening. "Will you, also, join your companion this day?" Michael asked, with his hand still on his great sword.

"Not this day." replied Chango. "My battle is not with you. It's with this traitor to my master. Time is on my side. He will falter and fall. I will be there when it happens. There'll be nothing you will be able to do then to save him when he steps out from under your covering. Remember this, Michael; the day will come when my master will be triumphant. All those who have opposed him shall become his slaves. Your supposed Christ shall be tormented forever. On that day Michael, we will meet in battle and you will be mine! Until then I will wait, patiently, for the opportunity and pleasure to destroy the fallen son of Shiva. Let all of creation be my witness! There will be no peace or rest for him until the day I fulfill my promise!" With that said, Chango vanished!

Michael smiled at the young man. "You do not understand your new nature and of what spirit you truly are. Young man, at one time you depended on your powers; which, to you, seemed so formidable and unlimited. You trusted in your own might and understanding. Yet, they all failed you in the past. Even when you supposed you were the strongest! They will fail you in the future! It's time for you to learn what true power is! Even Shiva, with his great power is limited. He is restrained to do no more than what he is permitted to by his God. The myth of the all-powerful Shiva is false! His God, who is known as Christ, defeated him on the cross at Calvary. He must obey the Spirit of God, bend his knee and bow to the name of Jesus, as does all creation! He must submit to the Word, for the Scriptures are a sharp as a double-edged sword, not only able to divide between bone and marrow, but between spirit and soul!"

"Young man, you must come to the full knowledge of the strength you have in Christ! You must learn to use the formidable spiritual weapons, which are available to you in His name and authority! Use these and no longer wrestle against flesh and blood! You must also put on the wonderful armor He has provided for you, since before time began!"

Michael looked at the former son of Shiva. At one time; was the most powerful witch on earth! With what to many seemed like unlimited power at his fingertips! Now, just a mere mortal, with no power of his own. How helpless he felt. He was no longer able to fight battles in his own strength. Truly, the young man was completely confused. All his weapons and protections were useless! He would never cast another spell!

Butch looked at Michael. His eyes filled with pain and frustration. But no fear! Butch finally felt a deep sense of relief. A great burden was lifted from his heart. He was grateful to Michael, "I thank you, sir, for what you did today. The fight was not yours, but you gallantly fought this battle on my behalf. With skill and honor you bravely fought in my place. Please, sir, understand, I am grateful for your intervention. But I must ask; what shall I do when you are gone and I'm alone? Most assuredly, it is then Shiva will strike. If not personally, then it will be through one of his slaves. Kind sir, you will not always be with me. You cannot fight every battle for me. How do I stand? How do I resist Shiva and his spirit and power?"

"You will have no need of anyone to fight for you." Michael assured him. "In fact, when you are filled with God's Spirit and the gifts of the Spirit are working through you; then you will, clearly, understand the battle is the Lord's! You will come to rest in Him. You will know He is your shield and buckler. He is your strong tower and your deliverer. You are his seed, his DNA. He has adopted you as a son into the beloved of God! In His will you will fight with all the invincible power of His heavenly hosts!" As Michael laid his hand on the young man's shoulder, the Spirit of the Lord filled him to overflowing! "Be strong in the Lord and in the power of His might! Lean not on your own understanding. Trust in God! Humble your self and He shall lift you up! He will establish your way! He will light and make clear the path for you to travel! *El Melech Ne'eman*"

With a tender smile, Michael vanished! Butch dropped to his knees and lowered his head to the ground. He began to pray to his Father. "Oh, Mighty Lord, there is so much I don't understand. I need you more than I can know. Do not forsake me; neither take your Spirit from me! Let me be pleasing in your sight, oh, my Lord, my God, my Redeemer!" Unknown to Butch, three beings watched as he prayed! One giant was the great warrior giant, Michael .The other giant was his battle proven companion; known as **Chironia**.

But in the midst of the two giants stood another figure, not as large as the two warriors; but, far more powerful! He was the Lamb of God, slain from the foundation of the world! The Great I AM. The Alpha and Omega. The Prince of Peace. Everlasting Father, Immanuel, Jesus Christ, Lord of lords King of kings! The two angels gazed at their loving Master and Michael spoke, "Lord, the journey will be long and hard for him. He will suffer much heartache and experience great loss. His life will be a constant battle. He will always be looking over his shoulders. Chango and others will not relent until their own end. The young man will be an outcast among some of the flock. Even some of those who will be his spiritual brothers and sisters will not understand."

"The religious spirit dwells in many churches due to their lack of knowledge and understanding of truth. He will always rival against the plans you have for the young man. Some will fear him. Others will doubt his conversion. They will slander him and desert him at times. What you've shown us almost seems unfair. You have blessed him beyond measure! But many will view his life in the flesh and consider his lot an unfair struggle. There will be few rewards in his life; yet great rewards in heaven. There will be many times he will suffer such loneliness. He will even doubt you love him. Like Peter he will stumble and want to quit!"

"Yes, Michael." shared their Master. "But like Paul, it will be hard. And before the end of his journey, his soul will be heavily scarred. But for every scar he receives on earth, for My sake, in My kingdom; I have prepared a crown in heaven for him. I have purposed many good works for this young man; for which I will be honored and this young man, My new son; My new creature in Christ will be richly rewarded in heaven! The enemy was right Michael. This young man was born to be a warrior, like David before him! But not for himself! He is a warrior for My Kingdom!"

"Someday he will be like Moses, leading many out of deception in these last days. When his time comes, Michael, you and *Chironia* will bring him to My warrior's reward. Now Michael, you and *Chironia* go! Watch, but do not interfere. He must learn to trust Me and learn. As he trusts Me and My Word, his faith will increase by leaps and bounds! By the will and power of My Spirit he will! The former son of Shiva, is now and forever the adopted son of the Most High God. *It is My blood, which saves mankind.* Because of My blood, he shall wax valiantly for My kingdom's sake! Amen. If My people will learn to have a relationship with Me than follow after man and traditions, then they will obtain knowledge and the riches of My kingdom. It is not by works; but by simple faith in the One whom My Father has sent. Seek and you shall find, knock and the door will be open to you."

This is not the end, but truly the NEW Beginning

If the Son; therefore shall make you free, ye shall be free indeed.
John 8:36

References

Astral Projection / Astral Travel

This is an of out-of-body experiences (OBEs) achieved either awake or through lucid dreaming, deep meditation, or use of psychotropic drugs. Proponents of astral projection maintain that their consciousness or soul has transferred into an astral body (or "double"), which moves en tandem with the physical body in a parallel world known as the astral plane. In astral projection you remain attached to your physical body by a silver "umbilical type" cord. Some people see the cord and others do not.

Athame

Some practitioners of ritual magic call this their ceremonial knife. In some traditions, the athame is a knife with a double edged blade and short (often black) handle; other traditions require that the blade be dull, curved, wavy, or a variety of other specifications. The athame is usually used for ritual and magical purposes only. The black handled, doubled edged knife is commonly used in witchcraft. It is strictly a ritual tool and symbolically represents the element of fire. The Athame is used to lay down a circle

Avastar

Spiritual warrior of great knowledge and power.

Baphometh

An image of a man with breasts and a goat head. A 'point-down' pentagram appears on the forehead, a *sigil*. Sometimes associated with the word "Leviathan" or lying spirit. This symbol has been associated with Freemasons, Knights Templar and Satanists.

Book of Shadows

A collection of rituals, teachings, recipes, spells, lore, songs, and invocations. This is the occultist's personal notebook / workbook of magical practices. A famous 'book' of this type is The Grimoire of Lady Sheba. Depending on their particular religious tradition, there may be texts considered "scriptural," such as passages from Aradia, or Gardner and Valiente's "Charge of the Goddess," or "The Laws" ("Ordains") that are held as rules within the Gardnerian and Alexandrian traditions.

Chango

God of Thunder, one of the Orisha of Santeria.

Familiar

Familiar is an animal kept as a vessel for the witch. In early modern English witchcraft, a **familiar spirit**, commonly called **familiar** or **imp** is a spirit who obeys a witch, conjurer, or other users of the supernatural, and serves and helps that person. Although they may not be as intelligent as their masters, they are often as intelligent as the average human. Familiars often perform domestic duties and help in farming, but also aid the person in bewitching people. If they look like ordinary animals, they can be used to spy on their masters' enemies. These spirits are also said to be able to inspire artists and writers (compare with muses). Some reclusive wizards rely on familiars as their closest friends.

Hecate

The three faced Goddess of the Witches; the maiden, the mother and the crone. It also represents three stages of growth of witchcraft; which are portrayed in the Greek as the three headed goddess; head of a lion, dog and a horse. Mother of a vampire.

Hunters

Those so devoted, so possessed by another spirit they can 'change physical shape' at will. Sometimes called 'shape-shifters,' or 'skin walkers.' Others call them werewolves, werebears, werecats, werelions, etc. They are commonly used to brutally punish the disobedient.

Kali

Kali is a goddess with a long and complex history in Hinduism. Her earliest history as a figure of annihilation still has some influence, while more complex Tantric beliefs sometimes extend her role so far as to be the Ultimate Reality and Source of Being. Finally, the comparatively recent devotional movement largely conceives of Kali as a straightforwardly benevolent mother-goddess. She is usually associated with the deva (god) Shiva, Kali is also associated with many devis (goddesses) - These names of these gods and goddesses, if repeated, are believed to give special power to the devoted worshipper. She is the wife of Shiva.

Ola – Olo - olorun

God of the Sky- God of the Dead. One of the strongest gods of Santeria. Chief god of the Yoruba pantheon. Owner of the sky. Most powerful and wisest of the deities.

Sanheim

In Celtic culture, Sanhein, (*saw* – ween) the lord of the dead, supposedly called together all the souls of wicked people who had died. It is believed that on **Halloween**, the barrier between the physical and spiritual worlds vanishes. Allowing increased spiritual contact and activity. To appease the lord of the dead, people originally offered human sacrifices. Then switched to black cats because of their association with witches

Shiva

The third deity of the Hindu triad of great gods, the Trimurti. Shiva, along with Brahma and Vishnu, form the trinity of the Hindu religion. Shiva is the god of yogis. Shiva has many forms. Shiva is called the Destroyer (of evil), but has also the aspect of regeneration. One of his forms is a panther. As destroyer, he is dark and terrible, appearing as a naked ascetic accompanied by a train of hideous demons, encircled with serpents and necklaces of skulls. As auspicious and reproductive power, he is worshipped in the form of the shivling or shiva linga (lingam). Shiva is depicted as white, with a dark-blue throat, with several arms and three eyes. He carries a trident and rides a white bull. His consort is Parvati (Devi). Lord of intoxidents and poisons. Shiva is the keeper of secret occult knowledge and power for which he is worshipped by yogis and demons alike. Shiva dances both the joy of being and the dance of doom but in every aspect, he breaks through the false ego to reveal the true self-lion within.

Strega – Stregheria, or *La Vecchia Religione*

Most people, who follow a pagan path, follow one whose roots are based in Celtic or British legends. The Celts have a very rich tradition and their religion spread all through northern and Western Europe. Druidism and Wicca, as it is commonly known, have their roots in this tradition. But when one uses the term "Wicca", it should not be used to apply to all of Pagan-kind. While for the most part, all Wiccans are Witches, not all Witches are Wiccan.

Stregheria is a good example. Stregheria, or *La Vecchia Religione*, the Old Religion, is Italian Witchcraft. The Tradition, as it is known today; began in the mid-14th Century with the teachings of Aradia, the Holy Strega. This was based upon a much earlier system of beliefs, dating back to the pre-Etruscan Italians. It is now, as it was then, a worship of the Source of All Things, through the personification of the

212

Goddess and God. Family and tradition play a major role in the lives of the Strega, and this is what gives this Tradition its strength and lasting power.

Sword

The sword is a tool for sovereignty and authority and like the Athame in use. It also, symbolically represents fire and the male aspect.

Ritual verses Relationship
The boy was seeking relationship with God and not ritual

Rom 10:9-13

[9]that if you confess with your mouth the Lord Jesus and believe in your heart that God has raised Him from the dead, you will be saved. [10]For with the heart one believes unto righteousness, and with the mouth confession is made unto salvation. [11]For the Scripture says, *"Whoever believes on Him will not be put to shame."* [12]For there is no distinction between Jew and Greek, for the same Lord over all is rich to all who call upon Him. [13]For *"whoever calls on the name of the LORD shall be saved."*

Phil 2:13

[1]For God is working in you, giving you the desire to obey Him and the power to do what pleases Him.

1 John 2:1-2

[1] My little children, these things I write to you, so that you may not sin. And if anyone sins, we have an Advocate with the Father, Jesus Christ the Righteous. [2]And He Himself is the propitiation for our sins, and not for ours only but also for the whole world.

1 John 5:19-21

[19]We know that we are of God, and the whole world lies *under the sway of* the wicked one.

[20]And we know that the Son of God has come and has given us an understanding, that we may know Him who is True; and we are in Him who is True, in His Son Jesus Christ. This is the True God and eternal Life.

[21]Little children, keep yourselves from idols. Amen.

James 1:20-21

20For man's anger does not bring about the righteous life that God desires. 21Therefore, get rid of all moral filth and the evil that is so prevalent and humbly accept the Word planted in you, which can save you.

1 Tim 2:3-7

3For this *is* good and acceptable in the sight of God our Savior, 4who desires all men to be saved and to come to the knowledge of the truth. 5For *there is* one God and one Mediator between God and men, *the* Man Christ Jesus, 6who gave Himself a ransom for all, to be testified in due time, 7for which I was appointed a preacher and an apostle — I am speaking the truth in Christ *and* not lying — a teacher of the Gentiles in faith and truth.

About the Author

Henry Lewis has an evangelical teaching ministry called
"Restoration Global Ministries."

Henry's heart and vision is to reach out to this generation and share with them that there is a real spiritual world and a God who really loves them.

RGM is an interdenominational, apostolic and prophetic ministry that offers faith, testimony, vision, and biblical teaching in order to bring spiritual authority and transformation from the Kingdom of God to you and to your city.

Henry is a national and international speaker with numerous guest appearances on major television networks, radio programs, conferences and churches.

His frequent media guest spots enable him to continue to share his testimony of how God can change anyone by the power of prayer.

Charisma Magazine, Oct 2000 shared Henry's Testimony

On June 26, 2007 - VOICE MAGAZINE
(Prophetic Revelation for the Apostolic Revolution)
released news that this new book would be printed on the handbill which was given to 7000 leaders for the Washington Israel Conference in DC.
July 16 -19 2007.

Voice Magazine has this book advertised in their magazine and on their online book store.

For correspondence:
http://theunholyanointing.blogspot.com
drhenrylewis@gmail.com
~~(805) 357-2390~~   ~~(770) 884-6310~~
~~E-Fax: (305) 489-572~~

www·halewis.org
229-226-4930